I0772920

ALAN VAN ORMER

Hidden in the Book

Book 2: Mountain Ridge Mysteries

Alan Van Ormer

ISBN-13: 978-1-962168-99-1

Chapter 1

"It seems like the gang is breaking up."

Chase Connor turned to the voice of Jake Myer who brought him a beer. "Why would you say that?"

Jake leaned against the bar and wiped it down with a towel. "Willis and Allison are the only two left of the group. They used to come in once in a while but not much anymore."

They both turned when a man with blond hair and wire-rimmed glasses walked in with a red-haired beauty, who stood taller than him.

"Well, look who's here," Chase said. "My old law-school buddy from Stanford—Glen Allan Pitts, in the flesh."

Jacob nodded. "Quite a couple. He'll need to get some lifts for his shoes with his paralegal, Penelope Busch, from Denver. They must grow them tall there."

Chase set his beer down. "I get educated every time I come in here."

Jacob laughed. "I should get back to work and

serve people who actually want to drink, not these slackers whose beer lasts for hours." He rolled his eyes with a grin.

Chase laughed. After Jacob left, Allison Winters walked through the door, her eyes darting around the bar. She was probably looking for her long-time beau, Willis Shepherd. When she saw Chase, she hurried over with a smile and slid down beside him. "Do you always sit by yourself, Chase?"

He took a sip of his beer. "It seems that way. What happened to Willis?"

"He called it a night, and I told him I'd find my own way home. Willis and I are going different ways."

He shrugged. "I could give you a ride home."

She nodded. "If not, I'll call an Uber. No worries." Her head bobbed to the music. "Would you dance with me?"

"Are you sure that's appropriate?"

She smiled. "It's just a dance."

The two joined the other couples on Mountain Ridge Bar and Grill's dance floor. Allison cut a glance at Chase as he whirled her around. "How's it going in the bookstore and antique shop?"

"Actually, I'm doing fairly well. I've been interviewing prospects to take over as managers of the two stores. I have a couple I'm interested in and asked them to come in for a second interview."

The two stepped up their pace as the music changed. "What is happening with you and Willis?"

She lifted her head from his shoulder. "I don't really know. His father is pressuring him to take over one of his car dealerships in Denver, and I know he's thinking about it. He wants to run the dealership here in

Mountain Ridge, so he and his dad continue negotiating. My guess is Nathan will give in with stipulations. What they are I have no clue. I just know Willis's father needs to make sure everything goes his way. Usually, Willis follows along like a faithful puppy, but this time he's actually sticking to his guns."

He spun her around. "What do you think about it all?"

Allison blew out a breath. "I really don't know what to think about it all. Part of me is tired of Willis, his parents, and their antics."

"Then why don't you break up with him?"

The music stopped, and they walked off the floor. Chase peered into her eyes. "Would you like to get out of here?"

She smiled. "What did you have in mind?"

"We could walk the few blocks to my apartment, or we could drive to yours."

"Your apartment it is."

After he paid his bill, they walked down the street toward the bookstore, the second floor of which Chase had remodeled into an apartment.

She locked her arm with his. "What are you thinking about?"

"Just how tired I am of snow," he said.

"You'll get used to it."

"Don't you worry about someone saying something to Willis about seeing us together?"

"No. People love to gossip, but they also don't like the Shepherds, so I'm safe. It really doesn't matter anyway."

"What do you mean?"

"Nothing."

Chase unlocked the bookstore door, and they walked upstairs. He opened the door of the apartment, and she preceded him into the cozy living room.

"You've done great things with this place. It's small but homey.

"Do you want a glass of wine?"

"I'd love one," she said, taking off her coat. Chase joined her on the couch. He handed her a glass of wine.

"Very good." She took a sip then set it on a table next to her. He wrapped his arm around her. "This is nice," she said, holding his hands.

"It is relaxing, but then it helps that you're here."

She lifted her eyes toward him. "You mean that, don't you?"

He tasted his wine and set it down. "I do. You're enjoyable to be with, I love your smile and everything about you."

"I feel much the same way about you." She sat up. "Could you excuse me for a moment?"

"Is everything okay?"

"Everything's fine."

~

Allison hurried into the bathroom, then reached into her bag to check her birth control pills. Damn it, she couldn't remember if she took one this morning. But then that was her normal time she took it, so she must have. She returned to the living room and dropped on the couch next to Chase. "Now where were we?"

He reached over, took her in his arms, and kissed her.

At first she responded, but then she sat up and peered into his eyes. "We're at the point of no return. There's no turning back. Is this what you want?"

"How do you feel?"

She stood up, took his hand, and led him into the bedroom.

His eyes widened as he let her lead him. "I guess that shows me how you feel."

Allison reached over for her cell phone and saw it was twelve-thirty. She lay in Chase's arms and rubbed his chest. "That was amazing."

"Where do we go from here?"

She lifted her eyes to see him. "Where do you want it to go?"

"This can't be a one-night stand."

She kissed his eyelids. "This was never going to be a one-night stand. I have feelings for you."

"Ditto."

She lay back down on him. "Then everything's fine."

Chase raised her head up. "What do you mean everything's fine? We've been sneaking behind Willis's back for the past two months and nothing has changed."

"But this is the first time we made love, and I told myself once that happened, it would prove our love for each other. You're not the type of guy who sleeps around."

He grinned. "Maybe I just wanted to sleep with you."

She rolled on top of him and smiled. "Right." It was an hour later when the two lay on the bed holding each other. She rubbed his chest. "I could get used to this." A few minutes later she sat up. "I should get going. I don't have clothes for tomorrow, and it's an early morning." She slipped on her clothes. "Let's go. I still need a ride home."

"Oh, right," he said.

The climbed in his Jeep, and they headed along Smith Lake toward Kila, where Allison lived. Except for the music blaring from the radio, they rode in silence.

Allison peered out the window. "Hey, pull over here."

Chase pulled off the road onto the side of the road. "Is everything okay?"

She turned to him. "You need to quit asking that because when I'm with you, everything is wonderful. I just wanted to talk to you a bit before you took me home."

"And we couldn't do that at my apartment?"

She grinned. "There's a place for everything, and at your apartment, we had more important things to do." Allison put her arms around Chase's neck and kissed him. "For the last two months, I've been wishing this night would happen, and now it has. I have wanted to break it off with Willis because I'm afraid of his father, but after tonight, I'm ready to end it with Willis. You're the only one I want in my life." She took a deep breath. "I know about your feelings about past gals you've been with—how you were worried about screwing their lives up, but please don't feel that way about me. You can't screw my life up."

"Why would you ever believe I'd do that?"

She grinned. "Come on, I've been with Willis Shepherd for close to two years. Now that's a screwed-up individual who holds onto his father's coattails to get where he's going. I'm just as messed up for staying with him as long as I have." Allison started to say something more, then stopped. "Whoa, what is that? Something just fled from the ditch."

~

Chase turned to where Allison was pointing out the window at something moving fast. "I don't know whether it's an animal or a person." He grabbed a flashlight, slipped out of the car, and approached the ditch where'd they seen movement. A man looked up when Chase shined a flashlight on him.

He hollered back to Allison. "Bring my backpack."

Allison joined Chase with it. "What is it?"

"It's a man, and he's bleeding profusely. Grab whatever you can so I can try to stop the bleeding and call 9-1-1."

She did as he asked, putting the phone on speaker.

"This is 9-1-1. What is your emergency?"

"A man is bleeding badly along the Smith Lake road. Please hurry."

Chase was doing what he could to stop the bleeding. He glanced up at Allison. "It's like something took a bite out of his neck. Grab a flashlight out of the backpack to see if you can find out where he went." He watched as Allison shined the flashlight out into the mountain area.

"There it is," she said. "It's just standing there watching us. From this distance it looks huge." Chase peered up at where she was shining. "What is that thing?"

Chapter 2

The ambulance arrived within ten minutes. Two EMTs jumped out and rushed over to Chase. One dropped down next to him and checked the man's pulse. "Very weak," he said. He looked at Chase. "We'll take over from here."

Chase ambled over to Allison who was hovering near the Jeep.

"What is happening?" She was shaking. Chase grabbed a blanket and wrapped it around her. "This will help you."

"Thanks."

The two watched as the EMTs did their work. One of the men said, "I think we've got him stable enough so we can get him to the hospital." Chase and Allison turned when they saw a flashing light. The sheriff's squad car pulled onto the side of the road. A deputy hurried over to the EMTs, talked to them for a moment, then turned and strode over to Chase and Allison.

"Allison Winters, what are you doing out at this time of night?"

"Just heading home from the bar and grill when we saw this creature. I can't even explain what it was, leaning over in the ditch. He looked up, saw the Jeep lights, and dashed off up the mountain."

The deputy turned to look at where she was pointing. He shined his flashlight in that direction. "I don't see anything now."

"It was there," Chase said.

The deputy eyed the two of them. "How much have you had to drink?"

Chase sighed. "One beer, but I'm as sober as can be, and there was something there."

The deputy turned to Allison. "And you?" She thought for a moment. "Three or four, but that was a while ago."

"I'll have to do an alcohol test."

Chase jumped in. "For what reason? She wasn't driving, and there was no accident. If you want to give me a breathalyzer test, okay, but leave her out of it."

The deputy turned to him. "Are you an attorney?"

"You might say that. The bottom line is, you have no reason to run a breathalyzer on her because she wasn't driving. We saw something, got out to help the guy, and saw something run up into those mountains. Instead of worrying about whether we're drunk or not, figure out what that thing is."

The deputy glared at Chase. "Mister, I don't know who you are, but watch your tone."

"Deputy, enough." They all turned to Sheriff Portal's voice. "What do we have here?" The deputy explained what had transpired. The sheriff turned to look at the location where Chase and Allison had seen the creature run to. He turned back to the deputy. "Let's take a look. Chase, do you feel like joining us?"

He nodded. "Could you make sure Allison gets checked over? She is shaken up about seeing it."

Allison touched Chase's arm. "I'll be fine."

"Please, have the doctor check to make sure."

The sheriff waved for one of the EMTs to join him. "How's he doing?"

He sighed. "I can't say but we're ready to move him to the hospital."

"Please take Ms. Winters with you to have her checked

over."

Allison took Chase's hands. "Please be careful."

He nodded and watched as the EMT walked with Allison to the ambulance. Chase turned to the sheriff's voice.

"Watch yourself, Chase. Willis Shepherd is no one to mess with." When Chase didn't respond, the sheriff sighed. "Let's go see if we can find Bigfoot."

The three headed up the mountain following a path that the creature had made. "Those are big footprints, bigger than anything I've seen," the deputy said.

The sheriff nodded. They stopped ten minutes later at the top of the mountain and searched the area. "Nothing," the sheriff said.

"There still are footprints, and they lead over the mountain."

The sheriff sighed. "My brother lives up there on the other side of the mountain."

Chase nodded. The sheriff led out. "Let's check it out."

The deputy followed right behind. "Why would you think he's involved?" the deputy asked.

Chase grinned. "Have you seen his feet?"

The deputy looked befuddled as Chase walked by him. "They're big," Chase said. Ten minutes later they arrived at the cabin.

The sheriff looked down at the tracks. "They veer off to the left."

As soon as he knocked on the door, there was heavy barking.

"Whoa, that must be a big dog," the deputy said.

Chase grinned. "Dunk is a sweetheart, just like the sheriff's brother." The deputy looked like he wasn't sure what to think. They all turned when the door opened.

"Chase Connor. Welcome." Silas Portal turned to stare at his brother. "What brings you up here sheriff?"

"A few questions for you."

"Come on in. I'd offer you coffee, but it's awfully late."

Silas glared at the deputy who was staring at his feet. "Do you have a foot fetish, deputy? What's your problem?"

Sheriff Portal took over. "Have you been here all night?"

Silas surveyed all three of the men. "Of course I have. What is this all about?"

The sheriff did a quick scan of the cabin before focusing back on Silas. "A man was seriously injured on the other side of the mountain, and the tracks lead to your cabin."

"Like I said, Lancaster, I haven't left the cabin since dinner. Check around if you wish."

The deputy started to look around, but he stopped at Chase's voice. "Sheriff, we can settle this easily by measuring the feet. Silas is not the culprit. Although his feet are big, they're nothing compared to whatever we're chasing."

Silas laughed. "My big brother is chasing Bigfoot. I told you he was up here, but you never believed me. Or is it a grizzly?"

Chase spoke, "It wasn't a bear, Silas. It looked almost human-like, so if there is a Bigfoot, that's what it is."

"Bah," the deputy said. "There is no such thing as Bigfoot."

The sheriff frowned. "Whatever it is we'll have to wait until morning to check more. I'm sorry about disturbing you so late, Silas."

"Always nice to see you, Lancaster. Stop by anytime." They all turned at the sound of a screech like an animal suffering.

"What the hell was that?" the deputy asked.

Chapter 3

It was the day of the grand reopening of the Mountain Ridge antique shop. Chase had moved the date up to the Tuesday after Christmas. Chase surveyed the antique store. He was happy with the renovations of the store. More importantly, Chase was proud he had purchased the two businesses and made something out of both. He couldn't visualize becoming a billionaire from what he'd invested in the two stores, but he was satisfied with the outcome.

He felt a soft touch on his arm. "Chase, they're ready for the ribbon cutting."

"Thanks, Gertrude."

Gertrude Bannon, the area chamber of commerce director, gazed at him. "Are you okay?"

He nodded. "Just thinking about what we were able to accomplish here." She nodded in agreement, and the two walked over to where the mayor stood, along with several council members and the chamber of commerce director.

The chamber of commerce's assistant rolled out light blue tape for Chase to cut with a large pair of scissors. Once he cut the ribbon in front of the building, the crowd entered and browsed through the antique shop to see what had been done.

"This is amazing," Allison said, standing near him with Willis. She turned to Willis. "What do you think?"

"Much better than what the previous owner had. Many

more antiques in the store."

Chase noticed a tall man outside with red hair with a camera shooting photos of the shop's exterior. "I have work to do. Check everything out, and there are refreshments in the corner." He left Willis and Allison and hurried outside to where the guy stood. "Can I help you?"

The man smiled at Chase. "My name is Dwayne Edmunds. I work for the *Mountain Ridge Gazette,* and I'm here to cover the grand reopening of the antique store. I'm searching for the owner, Chase Connor."

"That's me. I'll be able to help you. What would you like to see?"

"How about a tour?"

"Let's go inside. Please take all the photos you want."

The two walked through the door to the antique shop. Dwayne's eyes widened. "This is wonderful. You have the antiques organized by mixing old and new. For instance, that oversized vintage rug in muted colors anchors the space accentuates the modern furniture. I'm not an antique expert by any means, but that's a clever idea."

Chase nodded. "We've created a space that highlights the stories the antiques tell."

While Edmunds was shooting photos, he continued making comments. "I appreciate the blending of different period pieces that bring the space to life." He continued snapping photos at different angles. They continued the walk around the store. "You have so many nostalgic elements that evoke a sense of history including the vintage maps, the wooden display cases, and old clocks."

Chase smiled. "You know your antiques."

Dwayne shook his head. "Like I said earlier, I don't know a lot about the antique industry, but I didn't want to feel stupid when I talked to you." Dwayne stopped. "Thanks for the tour. I know you have others to talk to, so I'll just hang out and take some more photos, talk to a couple of people about my story, and not disturb you."

"You're not disturbing me. It's great you're here. Make sure you check out the showroom upstairs."

~

A couple of hours later, Dwayne sat at his desk at the *Gazette* downloading several photos from the afternoon grand reopening. He thought about the woman with the shag haircut and blue eyes. What a waste for her to be with Willis Shepherd.

Finally, he focused on his job. It was his first story on his first day as a managing editor. Now twenty-eight, after graduating from the University of Montana two years earlier, he was on his way up. He'd spent his first two years in a small-town newspaper in eastern Montana but jumped at the chance for the managing-editor position in Mountain Ridge. He turned his head quickly when the door opened and the owner of the *Gazette* popped his head in. "Good evening, Mr. Sanders."

"Dwayne. How was your first day?"

"I was a little nervous, but I think it turned out fine."

"I'm sure it did. Once you're finished, why don't you join the staff down at the Mountain Ridge Bar & Grill. It's our way of welcoming new employees to the newspaper."

"Thank you. I'll do that."

After Mr. Sanders left, Dwayne continued his work. After he found seven quality photos, he started on his article. An hour later he was finished filing the story and photos for the next day. He buttoned up his coat, put on his hat, and locked the door of the newspaper. The snow was coming down harder, and the wind started to pick up. He wouldn't stay too long at the bar and grill, but it was important for him to be there.

It was just before nine the next morning when Dwayne walked into the newsroom. Oscar, the layout and design expert, greeted him as he walked back to his desk.

"I have a couple of pages for you to proof."

It was only his second day at the newspaper and his first

experience at editing a newspaper. He was fortunate that his journalism professors had said proofing and editing were two of his strong suits, so that should help. He sat down at his desk, keyed his computer, and pulled up the first page, which happened to be a sports page. The sports editor always did his work the night before, since he did most of his work at night.

Later that morning, Mr. Sanders called him into the office. "Have a seat," he said. Dwayne did just that. "Congratulations, you've been invited to take part in the annual scavenger hunt at the Bernards on New Year's Eve."

"I don't understand."

Mr. Sanders sighed. "To be truthful I don't understand either because no one from the newspaper has been invited to their annual event. Each year, they invite three or four couples to their mansion. From what I've heard, it was built from scratch in 1897, has four floors including a basement and attic, as well as fifteen different rooms. In addition, there are hidden doors, stairways, and corner rooms that are locked."

"Sounds like fun."

Mr. Sanders nodded. "Anyway, the group will meet on New Year's Eve at five-thirty for a meal, and then the scavenger hunt starts. The Bernards will allow photos, and this will be a wonderful opportunity for a full-fledged feature for the next issue."

~

Chase spent the morning reading the book that the sheriff had provided him on the mysteries of Montana. He skimmed through the index and the back of the book when his eyes landed on the Bernard house. Interesting. Chase had heard some chatter about the mysterious house. He turned to the chapter. Strange happenings occurred at the house every Leap Year. Parties on New Year's Eve where things happened to guests. One year a woman disappeared for two days, wandering into the sheriff's office hallucinating about being taken to a spaceship. Another time a female guest was lost for a week, then wandered into a cabin wearing only her bra and underpants. She stated that she had been raped but couldn't tell the sheriff's department who it was or where it happened. The one thing the two had in common were needle marks on their necks. Their friends said neither had done drugs in the past.

Chase glanced at his cell phone and saw it was close to noon. He decided to walk over to the bar and grill for lunch. As he walked in, he noticed Dr. Boyd and his wife sitting in a booth. The doctor waved to him to join them. "How are things with the two businesses?"

"I've been busy," Chase said.

"That's wonderful news. It's picking up for me also."

They chatted for a few moments. Finally, Chase stood. "It was great to see the both of you." Chase found a place to sit. The server joined him quickly telling him the special was chicken noodle soup with a ham sandwich. "I'll take the special."

Once the server left, Chase thought about Dr. Boyd and his wife. He could tell Mrs. Boyd wished Chase would just go away, but Dr. Boyd wanted something from him. Then he focused on Allison. He loved the gal but could understand how cautious she was with their relationship. To put it bluntly, she was afraid of what the Shepherds would do.

"Mr. Connor, it's great to see you again."

Chase eyed Dwayne Edmunds. "Please call me Chase. How are things going?"

"It's going well. I wanted to do a follow-up interview for a story on the antique shop."

"I would be willing to do that. Have you eaten lunch?"

Dwayne shook his head. "I came over to grab a bite."

"Why don't you join me?"

He pulled out a chair. "If it's not a bother."

"No worries. The special is chicken noodle soup and ham sandwich."

"That sounds good."

The server hurried over to take his order, and several minutes later, the two were eating their lunches. Dwayne peered over at Chase. "It seems like you had a wonderful turnout yesterday at your grand reopening."

"I was pleasantly surprised," Chase said.

Dwayne finished sipping a spoonful of soup. "I'm surprised Willis Shepherd showed up to such a thing. The gal he's with is a knockout."

Chase tried to appear impassive. "Yeah, she's a cutie. They've been dating for a couple of years."

"She could do much better. I might just ask her out. Anyone is better for her than Willis Shepherd."

Chase finished sipping his drink. "Do you know the Shepherds?"

"I know that he and his father are businessmen."

"And powerful businesspeople in Flathead County. Nathan runs a major car dealership in this region and is expanding to other locations around the country. All I'll say is watch your step with the Shepherds."

Dwayne waved his hand. "I'm not too concerned."

Chapter 4

Chase was stacking books when the phone rang. He grabbed it.

The lady on the phone asked, "Have you ever thought of providing a taxi service for those who want to visit the stores?"

"Never thought about it."

"I'm a grandmother, and my daughter and I don't have a ride. We don't want to miss any of the sales you're having today."

Chase chuckled. "Provide me your address, and I'll pick you up."

Ten minutes later, he pulled up to the address, and two older ladies were sitting on the front porch. The house needed a painting job.

One helped the other off the porch. Chase hurried over to help both.

"Thank you, young man. Are you the owner of the antique store?"

"I am Chase Connor."

The younger of the two smiled. "I'm Waverly Kendall, and this is my mother, Belle."

"Nice to meet the two of you. Let me help you into the Jeep." Once they were settled, he climbed in, started the vehicle, and backed out of the driveway. He headed toward the antique store. "What made you decide to call for a ride?"

Waverly spoke, "We wanted to go yesterday, but we didn't have a way over there because my daughter was busy. She works at the newspaper. You may know Zoe Kendall. She's a receptionist."

"I don't know too many people at the newspaper."

Waverly continued. "She said she'd take us to the antique store this week because there are sales. We thought if we waited too long, we wouldn't get what we wanted, so we called."

"Makes sense." Chase pulled in front of the antique store and helped them out. "Enjoy yourself."

"Don't worry about bringing us back, we plan on spending a good portion of the day in town."

"If you need anything, let me know."

"We will, son. We will," Waverly said.

Chase parked the Jeep in the alley and entered by the bookstore's back door. Just as he walked in, the front door opened. "Can I help you?"

"I hope so," said an elderly man, hobbling with a cane. The man was breathing heavily.

"Here, how about I get you a chair to sit on."

"Thank you, son."

The man sat down on a wooden chair Chase brought him.

"What are you looking for?"

"I'm hoping to find some new mystery books. I've read all the famous authors but am searching for something new pertaining to the state, like the author who writes about Northern Minnesota."

"Got ya." Chase searched through the books in the mystery section. He brought a couple back to the man. "I don't have an author specifically writing about Montana, but here are a couple of local authors to try that have the Montana feel."

The man read the back explaining the book. "I'll try these two. Can you order books like the big bookstores do?"

"I sure can. Do you know what you're looking for?"

The man gave Chase some authors and titles, and he was able to order them for him. The man paid for all the books and smiled. "This is so great to have a bookstore like yours here in Mountain Ridge. It makes it so much easier for us old geezers who love to read."

"We continue to expand all the time."

It was close to closing time when Chase walked over to see how the ladies were doing. They'd been browsing for hours. "Are you ready to go home, ladies?" Chase asked.

Waverly shook her head. "My daughter is coming to pick us up. You might like her."

Her mother joined in. "It depends on if she gets her car fixed."

"What's wrong with the car?" Chase asked.

"I don't know, but it struggles to start in the morning, but she needs the car for work and for us."

They all turned when the door opened, and in walked a gal with strawberry-blonde hair, blue eyes, and a sparkling smile. Waverly grinned. "This is my daughter, Zoe Kendall."

"Mom, Grandmother, how did you get here?"

Waverly patted her daughter's hands. "It's okay. This nice gentleman picked us up so we could check out all the sales, and we've found a few."

Zoe took her mother aside and whispered to her loud enough for Chase to hear. "Mom, you know we can't afford it."

She smiled at her daughter. "The nice young man gave me a super deal and said we could pay him in installments. Isn't that nice of him?"

Zoe sighed and turned to Chase. "Thank you for helping my mother and grandmother."

Chase smiled. "We had a wonderful time. Is your car big enough for a desk?"

Her eyes widened. "No, I just have a compact car."

He smiled. "No problem. I can lock up early. Can you

help me load their antiques into the Jeep?"

Zoe nodded then turned to her mother. "That's just an old desk."

"No dear, it's an antique, and someday will be worth a lot."

Zoe sighed. "I'll follow you home."

~

She crawled into her car, stuck the key in, and tried to turn the engine over. "Damn it," she said, slamming the steering wheel. "I don't need this." She jumped at the tap on the window. She rolled it down and peered at Chase.

"I can try to jump the vehicle."

"Thank you." She popped the hood while Chase pulled the vehicle around to face the car. He hooked up some jumper cables, and she tried to crank the engine once more. Nothing.

Chase came around. "It must be more than the battery. I'll call someone to take a look at it."

"Thank you." Zoe crawled out of the car and walked over to her mother and grandmother. "I'm sorry about this," Zoe said.

"It's not your fault," her grandmother said.

They turned to Chase when he said, "I called Mr. Leopold, and he'll be right over to take a look at your car."

Waverly's eyes sparkled. "Ah, that's my daughter's boyfriend's father."

"Good to know," Chase said.

~

Chase was the last one to arrive at the Bernard House on Saturday evening. After having finished the chapter, he'd called to secure an invitation to the New Year's party. He rang the doorbell, and a woman with gray hair answered the door.

"You must be Chase Connor?"

"Yes, ma'am."

"I'm Vivian Bernard. My husband, Tom, is with the

others already."

"I'm sorry I'm late."

She smiled. "Dinner has not been served yet, so you're not late. Please join the rest of the group."

Chase followed the woman down a long corridor with photos of animals on the walls. Once past the corridor, they arrived at a living room area where everyone was sitting laughing and talking. They all stopped what they were doing when Chase walked in.

"Ah, you decided to join us," a tall man with long hair and a beard said, sipping a beer. "My name is Brink."

"I'm Chase. I'm running a little late. I had to help a customer who had car trouble."

An older man with long gray hair, square glasses, and a semi-lengthy beard spoke up, "Mr. Connor, you're just in time because dinner is about to be served. Let's all go into the dining room."

The group followed the Bernards to the dining room, which consisted of a large, oak table with oak chairs around it. The names of each person were on placards which sat on salad plates. A glance around the room showed a female-male pattern around the table. Chase noticed Allison's name was on the placard next to his. Where was she?

When Allison approached her seat and apologized for being late, Chase grabbed her chair, and pulled it out for her. She smiled at him. "Thank you."

On another corner of the table sat the man named Brink next to a gal who he called Bridget. The guy from the newspaper, Dwayne, sat next to a young redhead. The Bernards sat at the other end of the table.

Two servers brought in plates of food that included chicken, mashed potatoes and gravy, and peas. Wine bottles sat on the credenza. "Please dig in," Tom Bernard said.

"This is very good," Brink said. "I have always loved chicken cordon bleu."

"It's a popular dish, and one we've served each year

that we've done this. I'm sure you wondering why we plan a dinner and scavenger hunt each New Year's Eve." He wiped his mouth, took a drink of his wine, before continuing. "Our family has owned this house since the late 1880s, and we enjoy showcasing it to others around the community because of its uniqueness and historical value." He continued. "As for this party, we started it fifteen years ago after our son, Gideon, died. He was only sixteen at the time, and it was obviously painful for the whole family."

Allison spoke, "We're sorry for your loss."

"Thank you, Ms. Winters," Vivian said.

Tom Bernard's glare at Allison showed Chase he didn't like being interrupted. He continued, "And the scavenger hunt has been so successful. The way it works is we choose six or eight random people from the community, then pair them off with someone other than their spouses or significant others. The person you're sitting next to will be your partner throughout the evening." The host tasted his wine. "Mr. Connor, you haven't touched your meal. Is everything okay?"

Chase shook his head. "I'm good, just not hungry right now. I'll grab something soon."

"I noticed the same with you, Allison Winters. Are you not hungry either?"

She smiled. "I'm just interested in hearing what you have to say, so please go on."

After she said it, Allison grabbed Chase's hand under the table. He glanced quickly down at her hand as she squeezed his. He could tell something was bothering her. He turned back to Tom's voice.

"Back to the game. Each of you will receive three clues to solve the mystery tonight. If you do so, the partners will receive $25,000, a worthy prize. No one has ever solved the mystery."

"Why is that?" Dwayne asked.

Tom shrugged. "Who knows? But it hasn't happened.

Also, before you begin, we like to play a game of true and false."

"How does that work?" Bridget asked.

"We have six different topics that may or may not pertain to an individual in this group. It is up to you to determine that. It helps build camaraderie."

Brink interrupted, running a finger through his long hair. "Or it could destroy a relationship."

Tom smiled. "Only if you let it. Here are the six topics. True or false, one of you is an adopted child."

Everyone surveyed each other. Then Tom went on to another. "True or false, one of you loves another, but not the one you're with. Another true or false, one of you will never marry." Chase frowned. How could Mr. Bernard know the future? Was he that arrogant? And how could the last two true and false statements build camaraderie?

"Here are some more topics. True or false, one of you covered up a murder. True or false, one of you is a cheater. True or false, one person at this table had a liaison with an underage person."

"What is the meaning of this? How do you know any of this?" Dwayne asked.

Tom frowned at Dwayne. "I have my sources just like you do, Mr. Edmunds." He stood up. "I'll let you contemplate what has been said before the games begin. Once we leave, the doors will be locked and you will be in here until the sun rises. We wish you the best and hope that one group can finally solve the mystery."

Once the host and hostess left, Brink turned to the others. "This is really strange. What are we doing here?"

"We're searching for treasure would be my guess," Chase said. "Come with me." He took Allison's hand and headed to the foyer where he'd left his backpack. The two of them walked toward the basement where they were to start the search for the first clue—a card with the words, *'something solid.'*

"Not much of a clue," Chase said. "I have a feeling that's the way it's going to be all night."

Allison was quiet as they walked down the stairs into the basement. Once there, Chase tried to switch on a light. Nothing. "Reach into my backpack and grab a couple of flashlights."

She did so, turning on one of the flashlights and handing one to him. "You sure have a lot of stuff back there. It seems like you were ready for tonight."

He nodded, keeping his eyes peeled. "I read a chapter about the Bernards and this house. There have been some eerie things happening here over the years. People said they'd seen ghosts; others said they heard strange noises; but others believe that this is just an elaborate hoax."

"Do you believe any of it?"

Chase shrugged. "I don't know what to think, but I do believe there are things out there not everyone can explain. We'll find out tonight."

"Why didn't you eat any dinner? Were you not hungry?"

Chase stopped and pivoted toward Allison. "Partly, but there were a couple of gals over the years who felt like they were hallucinating at one of these parties, so I wondered if the Bernards had drugged them. My first thought was the wine, but then I noticed the vegetables seemed a little 'different'? Why didn't you eat anything?"

She sighed. "Because you didn't. I trust your decisions."

Chase stopped quickly.

"What is it?" Allison's eyes followed his gaze.

Slowly, he walked over with Allison hanging onto his backpack. "I think we found a clue." Chase squatted down on his knees to find a shiny coin.

Allison knelt down beside him. "Is that a gold coin?"

"It sure looks like it." He stood up and examined the coin. "It may be a Union coin. Could it be after all these years the Bernards have been looking for gold? And they're hoping one of these groups will be able to find it. So far it hasn't happened, but after seeing this, it's got to be right here."

Allison peered up at Chase. "That makes no sense. This house has been in the family since the 1880s, and the Civil War was over by then."

Chase's eyebrows furrowed. "I recall reading about Confederates who brought gold coins to Montana in the late 1860s. They wanted to resurrect the Confederacy up here, or I should say to start another war in the West. If I remember right, the stash of coins was worth more than one million dollars by today's standards. But they haven't been found. No one knows where the stash was buried other than the last time it was ever seen was in northwest Montana."

Allison's eyes lit up. "So, there's a possibility it could be in this house. Is there any way we can figure it out?"

"Not down here. We need to find a computer."

Allison sighed. "Let's take a look in one of the rooms upstairs to see if there's an office."

"Or maybe even books in a library would have information?" Chase placed the gold coin into his backpack. "Let's go."

The two made their way up the stairs into the living room area. "What's the second clue?"

Allison pulled it out. "Just as vague. '*Hidden*.'"

Chase rolled his eyes. "Wow. I think we've figured out the second clue since we found the gold coin wasn't hidden, but there has to be more that would be hidden."

Chapter 5

"Do you think it would have been down in the basement?" Allison asked, sticking close to Chase.

"I don't know. Let's see what we can find up here."

The two searched around the living room area, then went into an office finding an older computer. Chase tried to turn it on, but no luck. "Why doesn't it surprise me?"

Allison grabbed his hand. "Let's try the book angle."

They walked into another room, which turned out to be a bedroom.

"Check around," Chase said.

While they were searching, Allison spoke, "I'm surprised that they put us together tonight."

Chase grinned. "Were you hoping you'd have Dwayne as a partner."

She shrugged. "I don't know how it works, but what does it matter? And why do you have that grin on your face?"

"Nothing." He smirked and ambled away.

She turned him toward her. "Out with it, Chase Connor."

Chase shrugged. "Bernard wants to hook up with you. That's why he got you away from Dwayne."

"Hm, that may be a thought." She winked at him and took his hand. "Right now we have a mystery to solve."

Chase and Allison continued searching through the

house. "It's really strange that we haven't heard or seen the others," Allison said.

"This is a very large house with lots of hidden rooms, stairways, etc."

"I hope they're okay."

They climbed to the third floor and came upon a locked door. Chase reached into his backpack for a file and tried to open it.

Allison laughed. "Is there anything you don't carry in that backpack?"

After a few moments, they heard the door click, and Chase pushed it open. They stood staring in disbelief at what they saw.

"There are child's toys everywhere," Allison said. "It's like a mausoleum to their son who died." Chase picked up a toy, and it started chirping. "Ew. What is that sound?"

Allison screamed. "Chase, behind you!"

Chase felt a strong arm around his throat—a man's arm—then he felt a hand stick what felt like a pin into his neck. He tried to fight the hand off, but the perp was too strong.

Just then, the hand around his neck drew away, and he heard a screech as the man seemingly stumbled. He turned to see Allison standing with a baseball bat in her hands. They both watched as the man disappeared through a door he hadn't noticed before.

"Are you okay?" Allison said, dropping down beside Chase who lowered to his knees trying to catch his breath.

He grimaced as he rubbed his neck. "I'm fine. What was that?"

Allison shook. "It was a monster. Had to be at least seven feet tall. Did you hear the screech when I hit him?"

Chase finally caught his breath and nodded. "What was the third clue?"

Allison pulled it out of her pocket. "'*Is he alive?*'"

They both stared at each other. "He's alive," Chase said. He stood up. "Where do you think that door leads to?"

They both scrambled over to see if they could find a way to open it. Chase felt around the higher part of the doorway, while Allison did the same down below.

Finally, he heard a click, and the door pushed open. Chase stuck his head in with Allison holding onto his shoulders. "A lot of stairs. Let's go see who this person is."

Allison turned him around. "Are you sure? That thing looked like he could tear our limbs off without an effort."

He stopped and turned to her smiling. "No worries. You're here to protect me."

She grinned back. "You bet I am."

He started up the stairs with Allison holding onto his backpack, following right behind him. They made it to the top. "There were twenty-five stairs, which is more than what my parents have in their house in California."

Chase slowly opened the door at the top, and they stepped in. "This room isn't on any of the diagrams we've seen." They searched the room, and Chase found an old book. He blew off the dust, scanning the back index. "Here it is."

"What is it?" Allison asked.

Chase turned to page seventy-five and found what he was looking for. "It talks about Union gold stolen by Confederates late in the Civil War."

"What does it say?" Allison asked.

Chase scanned the page and stopped. "Hold it, listen to this. *'We were surrounded by Blackfeet warriors so we had to bury the coins quickly. We found a spot underneath a large shade tree, which helped us when we came back. We finally buried it, but it may be too late as the Blackfeet warriors had attacked.'* Then it ends."

Allison tilted her head. "Do you think this house was built over that spot unknowingly at the time, and then the current Bernards found out about the treasure?"

"A good possibility, and those two female guests must have found the treasure or part of the treasure." Chase frowned. "But that makes no sense."

"None of this makes any sense, Chase. I just hope we don't run into that monster ever again."

Chase slapped the side of his leg. "You know what I think? The monster is their son, Gideon. He never died but has lived in the shadows all this time, keeping watch over those who search for the prize. We must be getting close."

Allison took a deep breath. "Why would he try to stick you with that needle when you hadn't found anything?"

"Good question. Unless..."

"Unless what?"

Chase took Allison's hands. "The Bernards are always talking about games, and this is all one big game for their son. He knows nothing about the gold but enjoys the hunt just as much as the others. It could mean the others are drugged and asleep somewhere else in the house."

"Or worse!" Allison held her breath.

"Come on, let's head back down to the basement. My guess is the gold is buried underneath the floor."

"It's cement."

Chase shook his head. "Not where I found the gold coin. It seems like someone had started to dig there but stopped. For what reason, I have no clue. But I don't believe it's the Bernards who are doing the digging. Someone else found it, and their son took care of them, not realizing what he was doing."

Her eyes narrowed. "Do you believe they're dead?"

"I don't know. First thing we should do is try to find the others."

Chase took Allison's hand, and they headed toward the living room area. They both stopped in their tracks as they saw the others laughing and talking.

"Chase, Allison, join us," Brink said. "It's been a heckuva night. We've either been drugged or had too much to drink. Either way we're enjoying ourselves."

"Did you find anything?" Chase asked.

"There's nothing to find, Chase," Dwayne said. "This is all a joke. We've been trying to figure out what's true and what's not from everyone's information. What did you find?"

"Gold," Allison said.

"What?" Dwayne said. Everyone's attention turned to the two of them. "Did you say you found gold?"

Chase took off his backpack and pulled out the Union coin. Everyone gathered around. "It sure looks like gold," Brink said. "Are you sure it's not fool's gold?"

Chase shook his head. "I don't think so, but we'll need your help to get the rest of it."

"Let's check it out," Brink said.

Chase led them into the basement where they found the first gold coin. Once down there, Chase grabbed a shovel leaning against the wall and started digging in the area. The guys took turns digging, but after an hour, the deep hole they'd dug showed nothing.

It was close to three in the morning when Chase hit something solid. Everyone peered into the hole. "Is that it?"

"I'm not sure." Chase got down on his hands and knees and dug around the area with his hands. He finally saw something that read '*Union*' on it. "We may have found it." He grabbed the shovel, continued digging around it, and unearthed a large chest.

Brink dropped to his knees to help him lift it out of the hole. They set it on the ground right beside the hole and stared at it. "Is it—" Bridget asked.

"Let's find out," Chase said. He dropped down next to it, stuck a paperclip into the lock, and popped it open. A collection of gasps sounded around him as they stared at its contents.

"It's gold," Allison said. "And a lot of gold."

"What do we do now?" The redheaded woman named

Olivia said, peering at Chase.

Dwayne stuck his hand into the gold. "What do you mean what do we do now? We're rich. There has to be a million dollars easy there."

"It's not our money," Chase said.

"No one needs to know."

Bridget laughed. "Now, we figured out who the cheater was in the group. Is this how you got through school, Dwayne?"

Dwayne's face twisted into a scowl. "You have no idea what you're talking about."

Chase broke it up. "The gold doesn't matter if we can't get it out of here without the monster finding us."

"Monster. What monster?" Brink asked.

Allison piped in. "A large guy, seven feet or taller, attacked Chase with a needle, but we were able to escape. We believe it's their son, who definitely isn't dead."

"We haven't seen anyone," Olivia said.

"No. But then of course we've been drinking their whiskey and wine," Brink said. "Any ideas, Chase?"

Chase thought for a moment. "Maybe there's a way out of the room that wasn't on the blueprints."

Dwayne laughed. "You have blueprints?"

Chase grinned at him. "I read a lot about this place before I got here so I'd be ready. Dwayne, Brink, grab the chest, and let's see if we can find a way out of here before the Bernards show up." Chase led the way up the stairs toward the room where they found all the toys. It took them ten minutes to locate the right hall, and then the room. Once there, Chase took over. "Ladies, help me find another exit." They all checked the room from top to bottom.

Finally, when it looked like things were going nowhere, Allison felt underneath the fireplace and the wall opened up.

"Let's see where it goes," Chase said. The space behind the fireplace opened to a spiraling staircase from which they couldn't see the bottom. Bridget grabbed his arm. "Do you think it's goes underground?"

"It sure seems like it." Chase pulled out a couple of flashlights from his backpack and handed one to Allison. Then he led the way down the stairs. They traveled slowly for the next ten minutes before Chase stopped them. "Wow, it's a long way down there," Olivia said. "How much further do you think it is?"

"I'm not sure," Chase said, turning to Dwayne and Brink. "Wanna stop?"

Dwayne grinned. "We're not taking our hands off this gold. Keep going, Captain."

They traveled another ten minutes before they finally made it to the bottom of the stairs. What met them was a tunnel.

Dwayne and Brink set the chest down and sat on it. "Wow, this is heavy," Brink said.

"It should be because it's full of gold," Dwayne said.

The crew started off down the tunnel. It was fifteen minutes later when Chase thought he saw light. They all turned at a loud screech. There stood the man who had tried to stick a needle in Chase.

"You weren't kidding about how large the guy was," Brink said. "We had better get a move on it."

Chase joined them and they raced toward the light. Several times Chase, who was bringing up the rear, turned around to see how far back the man was. He was still following but at a more leisurely pace.

Ten minutes later they found the opening and scrambled out of the tunnel. Chase looked back to see the giant stop at the edge of the tunnel.

"He's never been out of the dark," Bridget said.

"That's good for us," Dwayne said. "Let's get out of here."

"I don't think so."

They all turned to see the Bernards and two other men who pointed guns at the guests.

"I'm glad to see you found what we've been searching for all of these years," Tom said. He turned to the men with the guns. "Grab the gold."

They went over to take the gold from Brink and Dwayne.

"What are we going to do with them?" Vivian asked.

Her husband shrugged. "Nothing but give them the $25,000 they won for completing the scavenger hunt. They can't do anything about us finding gold on our own property."

"I'd hate to disagree with you," Chase said. "This is Union gold, so it goes back to the government."

"I guess we'll have to disagree on that." Their host turned to walk away.

"Hold it, Mr. Bernard. Why did you choose this group?" Chase asked.

Tom pivoted to face the group. "Easy. Dwayne has always been a cheater, so if he did find the gold, we could bargain with him. Brink covered up a murder, so if he said anything about what he found, his secret would be uncovered. Luckily, we didn't have to resort to all that." Bernard's smile didn't reach his eyes. "Now for the ladies. Bridget was an adopted child, so she wouldn't know anything about the history of this place. All Olivia could think about was getting her hands on money so she could leave Montana."

Vivian grinned. "We knew if we invited you here, Chase, you would find the gold because that's exactly what you do—find things."

Chase laughed.

"What's so funny?" Tom asked.

"You forgot about the sheriff's department. I told them exactly where I was going, what was in the book I'd read before coming with the blueprints, and where we would come out. They're just a little late to arrest your group."

This time Tom spewed out a laugh. "I don't think so."

"Well, I think so," Sheriff Portal said. "You are all under arrest."

Everyone turned to see the sheriff and several deputies who stood off to the side. "I'm sorry we're a little late, Chase, but we made it just in time, or so it seems."

While the deputies were arresting the Bernards and the two others, Chase pointed to the cave. "There is a man over seven-foot tall that you'll have to bring in also."

The sheriff's eyes widened. "What?"

"The man is Bernard's son, Gideon."

"He's dead."

Allison joined them. "He's not, and we ran into him. The guy almost stuck a needle into Chase's neck."

The sheriff placed his weapon in his belt. "Well, let's go check it out."

They walked into the cave and there the man sat in a corner, crying and shaking.

When the sheriff pulled out his gun and pointed it at him, Allison touched his arm. "He's scared. Put it down."

"Are you crazy?" the sheriff asked.

Allison asked him once more, and the sheriff reluctantly complied. She moved closer to the man and started talking to him in a quiet voice. "It's okay. No one is going to harm you."

The man screeched, not saying an intelligible word, then jumped up and scrambled out the tunnel toward his parents. He wrapped his hands around Tom Bernard's neck and started choking him.

A deputy shot him, knocking him to the ground. Once on the ground, the big man started whimpering once more, rocking back and forth. One of the deputies pulled him to his feet and put handcuffs on him.

"Who the hell is he?" the sheriff asked Bernard.

"That's my son."

The sheriff's eyes widened. "He's supposed to be dead."

Tom sighed. "We were so ashamed of him that we told everyone he was dead, but he's lived in the house all this time, never coming out in the light of the day. This is the first time he's seen sunshine in many years."

Sheriff Portal shook his head and blew out a breath. "Take them all away. Now."

He turned to the group who'd spent the night in the house. "You're all coming downtown. We have a lot to talk about."

Chapter 6

For most of the morning, the six people sat outside the sheriff's office waiting to be interviewed about what happened. One-by-one they were called in. The women were interviewed first and then allowed to go home in the midafternoon. Two deputies stayed out with the rest of them to make sure there was no discussion about the evening amongst themselves.

Allison touched Chase's hand and whispered to him. "I'll talk to you later. Right now, I have a late lunch date with Willis. I texted him while we were waiting to talk to the sheriff. I have to talk to him about you and me."

"Do you want me there?"

She shook her head. "It's my task to bear."

The guys were there past dinnertime before the sheriff decided he'd gleaned enough information out of them. As Chase surmised, the gold would be turned over to the government, in this case, Flathead County. As they were walking out the door, Brink suggested they go to the Mountain Ridge Bar & Grill to grab something to eat.

Dwayne interrupted. "What about the New Year's Eve celebration the Shepherd family puts on?"

Brink snapped his fingers. "That's where we're going. Chase. Why don't you join us?"

"Sorry, but I'm going home to get some sleep. I'm tired."

"Your loss," Brink said.

Chase walked back to the bookstore. Within a block of the store, he was surprised to see Allison sitting on the steps, tears running down her face. He stepped up his pace. "What are you doing here?"

"Willis smacked me around because I wouldn't climb into bed with him. He also wasn't happy with me being involved with the Bernard event. I can't go to my apartment because he has a key, and I'm afraid he'll come after me."

He unlocked the building. "Come inside, and let's take a look."

Chase opened the door and turned on the light, then examined her face. "Wow, he did wallop you," he said, checking her eye. "Let's put some ice on it to help the swelling go down. Did you call the sheriff's department?"

Her eyes went wide. "Are you crazy? Willis's father owns the sheriff's department."

Chase sighed. "Let's get some ice."

The two went upstairs, and she sat on his couch. Chase went to the refrigerator, grabbed some ice, and wrapped it in a cloth. He brought it over to Allison. "Here, put this on your eye to help with the swelling."

"Thanks," she said, with a broken smile.

Chase sat down next to her, then rested his arm on the back of the couch. She leaned her head against his shoulder. "I was afraid something like this would happen. I wanted to tell him we were through, but I never got a chance because he was in my face right away, wondering why I hadn't told him about the Bernard event. Then he started kissing me. When I tried to break away from him, he threw me on the couch and smacked me."

Chase kissed her forehead. "You told me he was controlling, and that was definitely the case. Did you even think about jumping into bed with him?"

"Definitely not, especially after the other night with you. That was pure romance and love. With Willis there never was any romance. Just climbing on top of me, getting it over with quickly, and then falling asleep, snoring. What a life! Why I stayed with him for this long I have no idea."

Those were the last words she said, falling asleep in Chase's arms. He lifted her up, carried her to the extra bed, and covered her with a blanket. He sat beside her stroking her hair gently. "You're safe here," he whispered.

The next morning Chase finished putting his gear into the back of his Jeep for his trip to Helena to purchase an antique chest for the store. He had no clue what was in it. Allison had asked to ride with him, and he hesitantly said 'yes.' They drove toward Helena, which was three and a half hours away from Mountain Ridge. On the way, he planned on stopping in Missoula to talk to Professor Littrel about a book.

Allison broke the silence first. "Why are you stopping to see the professor at the University of Montana?"

"I want to talk to him about a book."

She smiled. "Oh, we're into books again, are we? One of the deputies told Willis that you helped solve a mystery by studying a book that was sent to the sheriff."

"That's right. It's a mystery book of sorts, and that's why I'm talking to Professor Littrel, hoping he has some insight into what it is."

"What do you think it is?"

Chase hit his blinker to pass another vehicle, and once he was past him, he continued. "My guess is it is a book that someone pieced together of unsolved mysteries. The compiler wants us to solve those mysteries."

"Who was the author?"

"Someone named Kitty Ladder."

Allison laughed. "What kind of name is that? Sounds like kitty litter. Hold it, I'm googling Kitty Ladder. You're right, the name Kitty Ladder does turn up, but it seems like it's a guy whose real name is Vincent Bullick. I've heard that name before." She googled the name. "He was the sheriff in Flathead County twenty years ago, then resigned after being blasted for not solving a murder."

It was close to ten when they arrived in Missoula. Allison typed the address for Professor Littrel's office into the GPS. They arrived at the building that housed the campus social sciences, found a place to park, and found his office on the second floor.

The white-haired professor peered up when they knocked at his ajar door. "Chase, you are here. Good to see you. And who do we have here?"

"Allison Winters, a friend of mine who is interested in antiques."

"Nice to meet you, ma'am."

"You too, sir."

He took his glasses off. "Now, Chase, what kind of mystery do we have to solve this time?"

"I'm not actually sure. An author named Kitty Ladder mailed Sheriff Portal a book entitled *Mountain Ridge Mysteries*. No clue why, but it did help us solve the Bernard mystery last night."

"I read about that in the newspaper this morning. You guys found gold coins from the late 1800s. Quite a find. I've also heard of the book, but not the author."

Chase nodded. "Kitty Ladder is a pen name for a former Flathead County Sheriff, Vincent Bullick."

"I've heard that name also. He resigned after a botched murder case. It involved the Shepherd family, if I remember right."

Chase sighed. "I know nothing about it other than what Allison had told me on the ride here, just basically what you had said."

Chase handed the book to Professor Littrel. "It seems that the book is full of stories of incidents that were never solved. The Bernard case is one of many. Sheriff Portal wants me to use the book to solve these mysteries that have never been completed."

Professor Littrel grinned. "Another mystery on our hands. I love it. Where do we start?"

Chase shrugged. "Maybe from the beginning. We have to run to Helena to pick up an antique treasure box, so I thought I'd leave this with you so you can take a look at that first chapter to see what you think. I've read through it and have ideas, but I want to see what you make of it."

"I can do that. In fact, I look forward to it. Stop by for lunch tomorrow at my house. I'll have my wife make one of her special lunches, and then we can talk. You'll probably be stuck in Missoula anyway."

Chase's eyes widened. "Why do you say that?"

"They're expecting a major snowstorm tomorrow afternoon through the evening."

"Ugh," was all Chase could say.

Chase and Allison arrived in Helena a little after noon. Allison laughed at the noise Chase's stomach made. He grinned. "My stomach is telling me it's hungry. How about you?"

Allison nodded. "I'll google and see what we can find." She pointed at an upcoming sign. "The Windbag Saloon & Grill is one of the food places on the exit sign. We can eat there." She quickly googled it. "Yelp says it has a nice array of lunch meals. This should do."

They pulled into the parking lot, headed into the restaurant, and looked at all the photos on the walls that displayed the history of Helena.

"It seems like all the restaurants in Montana have an elk head hanging on their wall," Chase said.

"It's part of the landscape," Allison said.

They found a round table in the middle of the establishment, sat down, and ordered a burger and fries. Once they were finished eating, they drove to a house just outside of Helena. Chase knocked on the door of the old house, and an elderly man with long white hair running down to his buttocks answered it.

"Can I help you?"

"We're here to pick up the antique chest," Chase said.

"Please come in. It's up in the attic. I haven't been able to get it down because the steps are just too hard for me, but my grandson is here to help you."

Chase and his grandson climbed the steps to the attic. "That's the chest over there," the grandson said.

Chase knelt down and opened it. "Dresses. A bunch of old dresses." Chase closed the chest back up, and the two lifted it off the floor. Chase stopped. "I'll go down first, and we'll try to slide it down the stairs."

The two men carried it down the stairs without any problems, setting the chest by the bottom steps.

Chase opened the chest and searched through it. He eyed Allison. "There's just a bunch of dresses."

Allison took several out of the chest. "Wow. These are selections of pieces spanning from 1940s western wear to 1970s denim and more. Quite a find."

Chase gazed at the older man. "Can I give you anything for this chest?"

He shook his head. "No, the former antique store owners my distant relative, and I told him he could have it when he was ready. He must be ready."

Chase placed the chest into the back of the Jeep. They found a hotel room, and once they checked in and went to their room, Chase took out his swimsuit. "I'm going to crawl in the hot tub, then grab something to eat. Will that work?"

Allison reached into her bag and pulled out a swimsuit of her own. "I had hoped we could spend time in the hot tub together."

Chapter 7

Allison was flipping through the television to see what was on when her cell phone rang. Willis. She hesitated before answering it. "Hello."

"You finally answered. I'm so sorry for what I've done."

"No, Willis, sorry is not going to cut it anymore. You can't continue to hit me, make derogatory remarks about me, and think it's okay."

There was silence on the other end. "How about we sit down and talk about it?"

"No, I need some space from you for a while to figure out if I want to be in this relationship. No, actually I've already decided this relationship is over. I wanted to tell you yesterday, but you were more interested in getting me into bed than listening."

"Did you run to Chase Connor?"

Allison sighed. "What if I did?"

"I won't allow you to hook up with him."

Allison could feel her temper boil. "You won't *allow* me? For your information, Chase and I have already slept together. And it's the best sex I've ever had." She closed her cell phone. Why did she do that? She'd just put Chase in the middle of their feud.

She peered up when Chase walked in and stopped at the frown on her face. "You must have just gotten off the phone with Willis."

Allison nodded. "Sorry, I really screwed up. I told Willis you and I...I'm so sorry."

"Let's grab something to eat and buy you some clothes." Chase disappeared into the bathroom, and came out dressed a few minutes later. "Are you ready?"

Allison nodded, then put on her parka and mittens. They walked down to a local restaurant, found a seat, and ordered Italian dishes. Allison went for a fettuccine and Chase grabbed some lasagna. Once the server left, Allison turned to Chase. "You're not going to say anything about me putting my foot in my mouth?"

Chase's eyes flitted around the room then came back to her. "It's true, isn't it?"

Her mouth dropped. "Of course it's true, but it's no one else's business, especially not Willis's." She reached for his hand. "There's something else on your mind."

"There is. It seems like I get myself into situations where I fall for gals who are either getting divorced or breaking up with another guy. I can't handle that again."

"I'm sorry I put you in that uncomfortable position. The difference is I love you and want to be with you. Did you know if your former girlfriends really loved you?"

Chase frowned. "To be truthful, I can't answer that."

She squeezed his hands. "I hope you're not changing your mind about me because of what I just said."

"No, I just don't want anything to happen to you. The guy's insane."

She smiled. "That's sweet, but don't worry. I know you'll never let anything happen to me. In fact, I've never felt safer in my life."

The server brought their food, and they enjoyed their meal, chatted, and laughed. After that, they headed down to a local retail store to buy clothes for Allison.

"What do you think of this shirt?" she asked, stepping out of the dressing room.

"It's wonderful if you want to show off your cleavage."

She took a deep breath. "I've always been told to show off what I have."

"True, but what would your boyfriend think if you were broadcasting them for everyone else? Besides there are many other beautiful parts about you."

"Good point."

An hour later she found what she needed, they purchased them, and they walked back to the hotel. Allison spent the rest of the night lying on the bed flipping through the TV while Chase read a book.

She clicked off the TV and rolled over to look at Chase who sat in a chair next to the bed. "You really love reading."

He lifted his head. "I do."

"What are you reading?"

Chase moved onto the side of the bed. He turned to the page he had been reading. "I've read these couple of paragraphs many times, and I know they have some kind of meaning, but I'm not sure what."

Allison sat beside him. "Maybe a fresh set of eyes can provide a new perspective."

He handed her the book. "Give it a shot."

Allison read the two paragraphs twice, then thought about what was there. "The paragraphs talk about a place where Flessie has been seen. How often does the county do land surveys? Is it every five or ten years?"

"I don't know," Chase said. He googled how often land was surveyed in Montana, and found that it depended on the reason for surveying it. He turned to Allison. "What are you thinking?"

"If they did a survey after this book was written, the boundaries may have changed, so the location of those two paragraphs may not be accurate. The author wouldn't have known that."

He grinned. "That makes sense. Thank you. That gives me something more to think about."

She smiled. "I'm glad I could help." She walked into the bathroom, where she removed her makeup and brushed her teeth, and came out several minutes later wearing a nightie she had purchased. Allison stopped when Chase gazed at her. "What?"

"I'm sorry," he said, lowering his head. "I just can't believe how beautiful you look with or without makeup on. And that nightie makes you sparkle even more than you normally do."

She blushed. "Thanks. I'm tired and am going to get some sleep. As much as I want to make love with you, I just can't because of what happened with Willis. I know it's not you, but I just need some time to get over it."

"Understood. I would never force you to do anything you didn't want to do."

She kissed Chase, then crawled into bed, rolled away from Chase, and was sleeping within moments.

~

Chase lay in bed thinking about everything that had happened over the past five months. He'd left California, left a six-figure job to come to Montana to run a bookstore and antique store. During that time, he'd met beautiful gals, only to have them dump him for other guys. To be truthful he did push them away because of his worry about screwing up their lives. In essence, he was screwing up his own life. Now, Allison was fast asleep next to him. He didn't know what to make of her and Willis other than he wanted to smack him around. Chase fell asleep wondering what would happen next.

The snow was heavier as they neared Missoula the next morning. Chase figured they were only ten minutes away from the Missoula city limits.

"Is it spring yet?" he asked Allison.

She laughed. "You'll have to wait a few months for that."

Just then Chase grabbed the steering wheel as the Jeep

started to slide down a mountain pass. He gently tapped on the brakes slowing the vehicle down a bit as Allison grabbed his leg. Once he got the vehicle back in control, he released the breath he'd been holding.

"We're spending the night in Missoula."

She grinned. "Someday you'll get used to the Montana winter."

He arrived at the Littrel household thirty minutes later, close to one. Professor Littrel was waiting for him at the door. "You made it. I was so worried because I heard the snowstorm has been upgraded to a blizzard."

Chase blew out a breath. "We decided to slide down into Missoula, but we made it. I've already decided I'm not going anywhere tonight."

"My wife has made up a bed for you two, so you're spending the night with us."

As Chase and Allison brushed off snow before they walked into the house, Allison said, "We don't want to be an inconvenience."

"Of course not," said a short lady with brown hair. "I want to get to know the guy who is just as crazy as my husband—digging graves in the Montana wilderness. Lunch is ready, so come and join us."

At Allison's puzzled face, Chase told her about their most recent case. He and the professor had helped solve a mystery involving the kidnapping of a Native American girl by digging into sites marked on a map from a book. Underneath the ground were the personal belongings of each of the girls. The sheriff was able to close the case because of the evidence they'd unearthed.

Once Chase and Allison had taken their coats off, they joined their hosts in the dining room. Professor Littrel grinned. "Gloria made her famous rustic Hungarian mushroom soup, which is a Montana favorite. Have you had it?"

"Never."

Allison turned to Chase. "It's a creamy mushroom that also has onions, dill weed, Hungarian paprika, and vegetable broth."

They all sat down to eat the soup with breadsticks. "This tastes wonderful," Chase said.

Professor Littrel grinned. "I'm glad you like it. Tonight, I plan on cooking elk burgers, pretty much the same as hamburgers but with a little tangier taste. I hope you'll enjoy it."

"I will."

After lunch they moved into the living room. Gloria brought out some iced tea, and they gathered around the coffee table to discuss the book. Professor Littrel brought it out. "Here you go, Chase. We browsed through the book, and I'm not sure if there is anything I can do to help you in this case. Many of the mysteries that are indicated in the book have been debunked, so there is nothing more that can happen with them. I'm sorry."

"Don't be," Chase said. "Just wanted to get your thoughts. I haven't read anything but the chapter dealing with the Bernards, and something came of that."

Throughout the rest of the afternoon, they sat around and talked, then after supper, the snow started to taper off. "You should be able to get back to Mountain Ridge in the morning," Professor Littrel said, before they all went to bed.

After breakfast the next morning, Chase and Allison drove toward Mountain Ridge. They arrived close to ten. Xavier, a high school student, happened to be in the bookstore, so he helped Chase carry the old chest into the antique store. They set it down, noticing people waiting outside for the store to open.

"Let's take this chest upstairs into the showroom closet area."

Once they got it up there, Xavier turned to Chase. "Milo said he'd open up the antique store."

"Good. I should go say hello to him." He hurried down

the stairs. Once he greeted Milo, Chase returned to the bookstore.

Xavier was at the cash register checking out some books. Once completed he asked Chase, "How did it go?"

"It went well other than running into another blizzard. It's getting old."

Xavier laughed. "I'm sorry, but it seems like you always end up on the wrong end of the snowstorm."

Chase rolled his eyes. "Get to work."

Chapter 8

On Tuesday morning, Chase and Allison were stacking some books in the bookstore when Chase stopped and stared at Allison. "Are you ever going to leave here?"

She smiled. "Not until you kick me out. I enjoy sleeping in the extra bedroom. It's peaceful and comfortable. No Willis. No Mr. or Mrs. Shepherd."

"You realize you'll have to talk to Willis sooner or later."

Allison shrugged. "I've talked to him several times already. He wants me back, but I told him I'm not going back. I'm enjoying working here at the bookstore."

Chase sighed. "I've been thinking about that. How would you like to be the manager of the bookstore?"

She grinned. "Seriously?"

"Yes, I am. You've been here for me the past few weeks, you've learned the ropes, and Xavier said you're a wonderful addition, so if you want it, the job is yours."

She wrapped her arms around him and kissed him. "I accept." They both turned when the door opened.

"Good morning, Sheriff." Chase wiped his lips.

"Good morning, you two. Let's go find Bigfoot. Your love life will have to wait."

"It's not that at all," Allison blushed. "He offered me a job and I accepted. That's how I show my gratitude."

The sheriff shook his head. "Today's generation."

As they drove toward Smith Lake, the two discussed what was in the book. "Several people have seen something in the Smith Lake area of the mountains," Chase said. "Especially around the northeast portion of the wetlands where things have happened. I'm not sure what, but that may be an area to check out. Where should we start?"

The sheriff grinned. "Emma's cabin, and she'll be a treat for you."

As they drove toward Smith Lake, Chase cast a sideways glance at the driver. "Sheriff, do you know a guy named Hendry Gilles?"

Chase could tell that the sheriff was thinking by his reaction. "He enjoys mystery. Was he looking for the book?"

"It seems like he was, but I have the book hidden in a safe place. I have read some more chapters, and this Bigfoot character we are searching for is in it."

The sheriff's eyes widened. "It is?"

"Yes, maybe ten or fifteen years ago, there were several sightings in the Smith Lake area right around the area we've been searching. There is an older lady who has lived in a cabin near here for many years. Maybe she has seen something? Also, the book mentions an empty cabin that is higher up in the mountains. Do you know of one?"

Again, Chase could tell that the sheriff was thinking. "There are all kinds of cabins in that area but empty ones. I can't think of any, but we'll have a look. Let's start by paying a visit to Emma." The sheriff grinned.

Fifteen minutes later, they arrived at the cabin. "Does it look like someone's there?" Chase asked. "It looks pretty abandoned to me."

"Let's go check it out." The sheriff drove to the cabin, parked the cruiser, and the two climbed out. He knocked on the door. A lady in her late fifties with red hair, wearing tons of makeup and thick glasses answered the door. "Emma Pitney, it's good to see you."

The woman smiled. "Sheriff Portal, did you come to

spend time with me? I don't think you've aged a bit since I saw you a couple of years ago."

Chase noticed the sheriff blushing. "You're still wearing plenty of makeup."

She laughed. "It helps with my complexion. What brings you out here?"

"We're here to talk about some happenings around here. Maybe you can shed some light about the subject since you've been here for several years."

"What do you need to know?"

The sheriff sighed. "We're searching for Bigfoot."

Emma spewed out a laugh. "If you were here ten minutes ago, you would have seen him wandering toward the empty cabin to the west. He made this awful screech." They turned to where she pointed.

"You had a good glimpse of him?" the sheriff asked.

"I did. He is over seven-feet tall easily, but he's not Bigfoot. He's wearing some kind of oversized snowshoes that makes it seem like he has big feet. However, he did seem a bit hairy, so he could be Bigfoot. Not my type of guy, so I didn't pay him any mind."

When Chase shook his head, she finally noticed him. "And who is this handsome young man?"

The sheriff answered. "Chase Connor."

"Aw," Emma smiled. "You're one handsome guy. Now you're a type I'd be willing to spend a night in my cabin with."

Sheriff Portal cleared his throat. "Thanks for the input, Emma. We'll take a look at the cabin."

After Emma closed the door, the sheriff and Chase headed back to the car.

"Strange woman," Chase said.

The sheriff laughed. "She is, but she is right. Many men, young and old, have spent evenings with her."

The two climbed into the sheriff's cruiser and drove the half mile to the empty cabin. "A guy named Johnson used to live here. He was involved with drug trafficking, but he was arrested and is spending time in prison."

They climbed out of the vehicle. "Do you think he would know anything about what is happening up here?"

"Possibly, but we'd have to drive to Deer Lodge to talk to him. He's been in there for a couple of years now and isn't expected out for another five."

"What happened to the cabin?"

As the two walked toward it, the sheriff explained, "He was just renting it. The cabin is actually owned by an out-of-state owner. I think his name is Jonathan Gartner."

Chase stopped and turned toward the sheriff. "Jonathan Gartner?"

"Do you know him?"

"I do. He was involved in a large drug trafficking operation in California maybe three or four years ago. Everyone associated with him went to prison, but he got off scot free because of my father and Gartner's money."

The sheriff frowned. "It seems enough money always buys a criminal's way out of prison. What do you know about Gartner, other than what you just told me?"

Chase thought for a moment. "Everyone knows he's into drugs and other stuff, but has been able to dodge the law because no one has been able to pin anything on him. As you can imagine, he loves money, so he could be part of the resort they've been talking about. My guess is this area would be the perfect spot to build a resort."

"You're right. This is the area they've been talking about at preliminary meetings." They started walking again. "I understand your father is coming to town in the next week or two."

Chase laughed. "I knew sooner or later he would become involved in the situation. He's all about making money, and resorts are right up his alley."

"Do you actually believe the resort will be profitable?"

Chase took his hat off, ran his fingers through his hair,

and placed it back on his head. "Sheriff, the only thing you need to know about my father is that he only becomes involved in a sure thing."

"But didn't he drop out of the equation after what happened with Shepherd and the kidnapping of the Native American girls earlier?"

"My dad will never deal with Shepherd again, but if there are new investors for a project, he'll listen."

They both stopped. "Did you hear that screeching? It's almost like the noise Bernard's son made," Chase said.

They rushed toward the cabin and watched as a large human or creature burst out screeching through the front door, then headed up into the mountains. "What the hell was that?" the sheriff asked.

"I have no clue," Chase said, "but it sure looks something like who Allison and I saw the other night—Bernard's son."

"Stay behind me." The sheriff pulled out his weapon, slowly walked into the cabin, and stopped. His face was perspiring. "What happened?" A form of a body sat in the chair not moving. The sheriff hit his mic and called dispatch. "Send crews out to these coordinates immediately. We have a killer on the loose."

Thirty minutes later, the EMTs checked over the body. "The man's been dead for several hours or maybe even days," one of them said. "We'll know more after an autopsy. It looks like whoever did this was just pulling out body parts like part of a game."

When Chase heard the word 'game,' he quickly grabbed the sheriff.

"What is it, Chase?"

"Outside, please."

The two walked outside the cabin. "Sheriff, Tom and Vivian Bernard continuously talked about games in the house where we found the gold. Remember Gideon is over seven-foot tall—looks like some kind of a freak."

"That wasn't him because Gideon's in a mental institution."

"Granted, but what if there are others?"

The sheriff rubbed his beard. "Are you saying that the Bernards hatched more of those creatures?"

"Not necessarily, but maybe someone associated with them did. There are at least two chapters in that book about Bigfoot. Maybe there is something I can find out of it."

"Okay, I'll drive you back, and you can do some reading tonight. First thing tomorrow, we'll meet for breakfast at the bar and grill."

They both turned when two deputy vehicles showed up. "What's up, sheriff?" one of the deputies said.

Sheriff Portal let out a breath. "There is a large creature loose in this area of the mountains, and we need to find it. The creature left one dead body. Be careful, it is dangerous. Also, make sure to warn those still living in the cabins about the creature. I'll do some searching in another area."

Once they climbed in the vehicle, the sheriff turned toward Chase. "Before I drop you off, we have one more stop to make."

Dwayne, carrying his camera, knocked on the sheriff's window just as they were about to leave. He opened the window.

"Sheriff, I heard on the scanner there was a death. What details do you have?"

The sheriff growled, "Come down to the sheriff's office, and I'll give you all the information you need. Don't go taking photos around the site."

"I'm just doing my job."

The sheriff sighed. "I understand, son, but I'm also doing my job, and if you go near the crime scene, I'll have you arrested. Come down to the station later, and I'll fill you in on what I can."

Thirty minutes later, the sheriff and Chase climbed back into the sheriff's cruiser. Once they were on the road, the sheriff said, "Hopefully, you can find something in that book to help us."

Chase nodded. "I'd also talk to the Bernards about the creature. They know a lot, and they may be open to making a deal with you."

The sheriff laughed. "Damn lawyers, always finding ways to get these criminals off."

Chase grinned. "Just trying to help. Remember, I'm not a practicing attorney; I'm just a bookstore and antique shop owner."

"Well, bookstore and antique shop owner, we're not done yet."

Chapter 9

The sheriff turned onto the road that ran around Smith Lake. "Let's try your suggestions. Where were the suggestions again?"

Chase sighed. "By the tree line above the cabin we just visited."

"That's where we'll start."

They found a spot to park near the tree line, jumped out of the vehicle, and made the walk up the mountain. "The snow on the trail is packed down, meaning animals or others have been along here regularly," the sheriff said.

Chase stopped, focused on one area.

The sheriff spun to where he was staring at something in the distance. "What did you see?"

"I'm not sure, but I saw something flash behind the tree line right over there."

The two hurried the best they could in the deep snow toward the spot where Chase had seen something. Twenty minutes later, winded, they came upon some tracks. "It's our creature."

Sheriff Portal took a deep series of breaths then bent down to the tracks. "It looks like they twist further into the mountains. Let's take a look."

For the next hour they climbed higher into the mountains following the tracks. "This creature travels awfully quickly for a big guy," the sheriff said.

"If he's a creature."

"What are you saying?"

Chase stopped and brushed some snow off his jeans. "It's hard to imagine that a creature this large hasn't ever been captured or even seen. I'm new to the Montana scene, but I've learned quickly that a Montanan has no problem pulling out a gun without thinking."

The sheriff laughed. "True, but even a Montanan can get scared. And right now, I'm scared because I don't know what I'm facing."

"I don't think he wants to be seen either, so it'll be difficult for us to find him."

Chase proved to be right. The trail stopped an hour later at a rock.

"Damn it," the sheriff said. "The thing can't just disappear without a trace."

"It seems like it has. Let's look around here a bit."

They spent another hour searching around but couldn't find anything. Finally, Chase and the sheriff sat down on a rock. "Do you think there's a portal or something like that in the area?" Chase asked.

The sheriff scratched his beard. "I never thought of that. I've heard of portals, but I'm not sure I believe in such a thing."

"There are things that are hard to figure out, so anything's possible."

The sheriff rubbed his stomach. "The one thing I know is I'm famished. I'm going to drive home, grab something to eat, and think about all of this. I'll drop you off at your place."

The two walked slowly back down the hill to the cruiser. "I'm out of shape," the sheriff said.

"That makes two of us."

They crawled into the vehicle and drove back toward Mountain Ridge. Sheriff Portal dropped Chase off in front of his bookstore. "I'll talk to you later. Have a good night."

"The same to you."

When Chase walked up the steps to his apartment, Allison was sitting on the couch drinking a beer. "I hope you don't mind."

"I could use one also." Chase went to the fridge, grabbed one, and joined her.

"No luck out in the barren mountains of Montana?"

He grinned. "Nope, but we'll keep trying."

"You and the sheriff are becoming quite close. Is that a good thing?"

"What do you mean?"

Allison finished her drink. "Mr. Shepherd owns most of the sheriff's department, or at least has them doing things he needs done. It just may be a little awkward if—"

Chase set his beer on the table. "With you being here?"

She nodded. He tapped her leg. "Don't worry about Mr. Shepherd or Willis. I can handle the two of them."

"I hope so."

He gazed at her. "You're really concerned, aren't you?"

"I am. I've been with Willis for a couple of years, and during that time, I've learned how mean his father can get if things don't go his way, and what I understand is that your family turned down helping the resort project because of Dr. Boyd's involvement with the Native American girls. He'll never forgive you."

He took a deep breath. "And all I wanted to do was own a bookstore."

Allison laughed. "Welcome to Mountain Ridge."

~

Allison came down wearing a sweatshirt, blue jeans, and heel boots. Before she headed out, she decided to spend some time browsing the shelves of antiques.

"Good morning, Allison."

With a gasp, she spun around. "Good morning, Milo," she said. "You caused me a fright." She smiled at a man shorter than she was with a crew cut, glasses, and wearing a tie with a short-sleeved shirt.

"Have you come down to check out what we have?"

"I have."

The old man's smile widened. "I'd be glad to show you around." Milo walked over to an antique dresser. "Could you help me move this?"

She hurried over to him. "I sure can."

They moved it to the 1900s display he was setting up. Allison stepped back and observed what he was doing. "How do you decide what you want in a display?"

"Have a seat, and I'll grab us some coffee so I can explain it to you."

Allison touched Milo's arm. "I can help."

He smiled. "Right this way."

The two went into a room in the back where Chase had put in a refrigerator, coffee pot, and several other snacks for patrons who visited the store.

"Have you ever made coffee before?"

Allison grinned. "Do I look prim and proper?"

He laughed. "No, but being with the Shepherds, you probably had a lot of people do things for you."

"I'll forget you said that."

Once the coffee was brewing, the two sat down at the table. Milo got up to grab some cups. "The most important thing about a display is creating an appealing arrangement with creative touches."

Once the coffee was finished, Allison poured each a cup.

"Thank you. I'm sorry about what I said earlier."

"Don't be. We don't know each other, but we will." When their coffee cups were empty, she took them to the sink. "Now explain to me how this display was arranged."

They walked out into the showroom. "As you noticed, I've arranged the antique pieces in groups of three or five. It's important because by spreading them across different areas it creates cohesive clusters. Customers can get a feel for what they might look like in their own homes."

He sipped on his coffee. "You notice there are some collections on top of antique wooden cabinets with glass doors. It's perfect for showcasing collections because it adds charm and provides a protected display space."

Allison ran her hand along a picture rail. "This is a unique way to display collections without cluttering surfaces."

"It is," Milo said. "If you notice I use hooks to hang vintage items like keys, hangers, and small signs. Why do you think that's important?"

Allison thought for a moment. "Does it add visual interest and utilizes vertical space?"

"Correct. Finally, displaying collections on open shelving allows you to showcase antiques while keeping them accessible."

Over the next hour, Milo gave her a tour of the rest of the store.

Finally, she told him she was going to see how Chase was doing.

Milo smiled. "Your smile is a breath of fresh air."

"Thank you. Chase made a wise choice in hiring you because you know what you're doing." She reached up and kissed him on the cheek.

"You're not getting fresh with me, are you?"

She smiled. "It's just if I knew my grandfather, I would want him to be like you." She hurried over to the bookstore, finding Chase stacking books.

"Good morning, Allison."

"Good morning. You're already working?"

He stopped and eyed her. "Shipments come in first thing in the morning, so that's usually the first thing I do."

"Do you need help?"

"If you want to help, that would be great."

Over the next thirty minutes, they moved the books around to the correct shelves. Allison turned when the door opened. Her eyes widened. "Willis, what are you doing here?"

"I wanted to talk to you, and I heard you were here."

Allison let out her breath. "I don't know if we have anything to talk about."

His eyes begged her. "Just give me a few moments to talk to explain what's going on with me. Please, just five minutes."

"Okay, let's go grab a cup of coffee over at the bar and grill." She turned to Chase. "I'll be back in a little while."

"Take your time."

Chapter 10

Willis opened the door for her, and they found a seat by the window. Jake, the owner, joined them, carrying a coffee pot. "What can I get for you two?"

Willis smiled. "Just coffee."

"It's been a while since I've seen you two together. Have you been out of town?"

Willis glanced up. "We've just been busy."

"I see. I'll bring you some fresh coffee as soon as it's ready."

Willis turned to Allison and took her hands. "I'm sorry about how I acted that night and am trying to figure out what I can do to straighten everything out, so we can go back to the way we were."

Jake brought steaming cups of coffee over. "Thanks, Jake," Allison said.

"You're welcome," he said, then hurried away.

Allison turned back to Willis. "That's not the first time that you've lost your temper with me. Afterward, you've said you were sorry and would change. I can't deal with your abuse and false promises anymore."

Willis sipped on his coffee. "We had talked about marriage, so maybe that's what is missing in our life."

Allison's eyes widened. "You're talking about marriage when you beat the hell out of me one night because I wouldn't perform for you in bed. Are you nuts?"

"Lower your voice," Willis whispered, looking around.

Allison stood up. "No, Willis, right now I can't deal with you. You've told me you're sorry, but I've heard that before. There's no way I'd marry an abusive husband. How stupid I'd be to do so."

He grabbed her arms.

"Let me go. You're hurting me." She saw something in his eyes she'd never seen before.

"Don't mess with me, Allison. You don't know what a Shepherd is capable of."

Allison didn't say anything, she just turned, and hurried out of the bar and grill. She stormed into the bookstore, ran over to Chase who stood by a bookshelf, and wrapped her arms around him. "Please hold me and don't let me go."

He did as she asked. Several minutes later she backed off and peered into his eyes. He wiped away the tears. "What happened?"

"He's proposing marriage but didn't tell me how he's going to control his anger issues. He then threatened me. I don't know what to do."

Chase sighed. "One of the part-time employees needed some extra hours, so she's here right now. Let's go for a ride."

The two grabbed their coats, then walked out to the Jeep. He opened the door for her, she climbed in, and slid over. "Thanks."

Chase closed the door, opened his door, and slid in. "Are you ready?"

She nodded. Chase started the Jeep, backed up, and headed toward Smith Lake. "Where are we going?"

"We're going to a cabin."

Allison reached over and took Chase's right hand. "Why are we going to a cabin?"

Chase turned onto the highway toward Smith Lake. "There's something we missed when we were searching for Bigfoot, and I wanted to check it out during the day's light."

"Isn't that the sheriff's job? And what does that have to do with what I just told you?

Chase squeezed her hand. "You're right, it is the sheriff's job, but my hope is it will take your mind off Willis. I'm also curious, and I want to know what is there. Besides, you wanted to help me find Bigfoot."

She sighed. "Yeah, I did, but I don't know if this will help get my mind off Willis."

He smiled at her. "Maybe. Maybe not, but afterward, I'll take you to a basketball game, and we'll eat popcorn."

She smiled. "A girl can't beat that."

Chase pulled into a gravel driveway in front of an abandoned cabin. They got out of the Jeep and walked over to the cabin. Suddenly, Chase stopped and spun to face a thatch of trees.

"What is it?" Allison asked, looking the way he had.

"I don't know. Just a weird feeling that someone is watching us. Maybe we should search around the cabin. Stay close to me."

They searched a thirty-foot radius around the cabin. Twenty minutes later they were preparing to enter it when Allison spotted something on the ground. "Wait, Chase, I think I've found something. It looked like something shiny."

Chase got down on his knees and started digging around the area with his hands. He peered up at her. "Can you grab a shovel out of the back of the Jeep?"

She did as he asked and came back with two shovels. "I can help." She grinned at his perplexed expression.

The two started digging around the area. "How were you able to find the glow in all this snow?"

"I don't know. Just thought I saw something shiny."

~

They dug for another five minutes and got down to the grass level. Chase dug again to get to the dirt. He lifted his eyes toward Allison. "This is weird. I can't get through. It's not grass; it's a rug made out of grass." He pulled on the edge, and it rolled up. "Wow. It's a locked shelter.

Chase pulled out his cell phone and dialed Portal. "Sheriff, we found something at the old cabin where we were looking for Bigfoot."

"We're on our way. Don't touch a thing."

Chase closed his phone and searched the area.

"Do you see something?" Allison asked, taking his hand. "No, but I still have this sense that someone is watching us, and it's eerie."

After finding nothing, Chase turned back to the cabin. "Let's check on the inside to see if we can find anything."

"Didn't the sheriff say to wait?"

He grinned. "He said don't touch anything around where we dug; the sheriff said nothing about the inside of the cabin." They stepped over the crime tape. He took her hand, knocked first, then when there wasn't a response, he opened the door.

Allison jumped back when a large bird flew out of the cabin. "What was that?"

"An owl, I think," Chase said. "It's still really dark in here. I'll grab a couple of flashlights." He had climbed into the car when Allison screamed. Grabbing the flashlights, he dashed back in. He froze at the sight of a body hanging from the rafters, except the guy was alive!

"Help me!" he rasped. Chase and Allison scrambled over to lift him off the hook.

Once they had him on the ground, Chase noticed blood streaming from the guy's shoulder just like it had on the guy in the ditch. "Looks like a bite mark." Chase had brought his backpack in, and he grabbed what he could out of it to stop the bleeding. He handed her a small towel. "Hold down tight on this."

Allison pressed the towel against his shoulder, while Chase did what he could to get him breathing by doing CPR. He grabbed his cell phone and dialed 9-1-1. "Man bleeding profusely, but still alive." Chase gave directions to the cabin.

Five minutes later one of the deputies came through the door. "What do you have, Chase?"

"We're trying to keep this guy alive."

The deputy dived down beside him. "Here, ma'am, let me take over."

"What do you have, Chase?" Chase lifted his eyes up to the sheriff. "Just like what we found in the ditch, but this guy is worse off. He was hanging from the rafter. I don't know if he'll make it."

The EMTs came scrambling into the cabin a few minutes later. "We'll take over, Deputy." They went to work.

Chase and Allison stepped outside with the sheriff. "What were you doing here in the cabin, Chase? What were you thinking?"

Chase peered at the sheriff. "There was something that didn't jive the last time we were here, and I wanted to come here during the light of the day. It's a good thing we did."

"I really should throw you in the cell for a night, Chase, so you can understand that we are law enforcement, and it is our job."

Chase was about ready to say something when Allison touched his arm. He turned to her, and she was shaking her head. Chase turned back to the sheriff. "I'll show you something else Allison found."

They went to the spot that they had dug up. The sheriff studied the situation. "It seems like an underground storage shelter, but why would anyone want that in the mountains? Let's see what's down there." He grabbed a crowbar out of his truck, lifted the lock, and snapped it. As soon as he opened the door, a loud screech came from behind them. They all turned to where the sound came from.

"What is that?" Allison asked.

The other two shook their heads. "We've heard it before," Chase said. "But we have no clue what it is."

Chase and the sheriff opened the door to the

underground cellar. "Let's go down and take a look." Sheriff Portal climbed down the steps with Chase and Allison following behind. He shined his flashlight around the room.

Bones covered the floor.

The sheriff quickly turned to the other two. "Don't touch anything. We'll get the task force down here to check everything out. This is really strange, but then everything about this has been strange." He turned to Chase. "Have you found out anything more in that book about Bigfoot?"

Chase nodded. "The people who have seen Bigfoot are not from around here. They were all travelers from other states hiking through the mountains. Also, most sightings were during the spring and summer. Very few during the winter. I can dig some more."

"You do that," the sheriff said.

"But right now, we have a basketball game to attend. Xavier is all excited about his boss watching him play. I have no clue why, other than he considers me a big brother."

Chapter 11

"I was a junior the last time I was at a high school basketball game," Allison said as they watched the teams warm up. "A bunch of us sat under the basket and cheered on the boys basketball team. Of course, we were only there to check out the guys' legs."

"Like those?" Chase asked.

Allison giggled. "There weren't as many guys with ostrich legs as there are now. Wow, look at the muscles on that guy's legs?" They both laughed. "This is nice just to go out together, doing something fun," Allison said. She shifted closer to Chase and locked arms with him. "Thank you for inviting me."

"Xavier is the one who actually invited us."

"True."

They turned when members of the Boyd family sat below them. Allison quickly released his arm.

"Chase, you're at a basketball game?" Clementine looked over her shoulder.

"Yep, I thought it would be fun to see how the high school kids play today."

Clementine grinned. "Number forty-four is a good basketball player. Watch him."

Her mother frowned. "Clementine, the boy is only an eighth grader. He probably won't play much."

"That's okay; he's still cute."

Mrs. Boyd peered up at Chase. "What are you doing here, Allison? What happened to you and Willis?"

Allison sighed. "Chase is my boss and we try to be involved in as many community activities as possible. As for Willis, we're working things out."

Mrs. Boyd turned back to Chase. "I'm glad your father was able to prove that Darren had nothing to do with the kidnapping of the Native American girls."

"I'm sure you're happy," Chase said.

"No help from you." She shifted away from him.

Allison frowned and whispered in his ear. "I'm sorry." Chase just shrugged.

The game started five minutes later. Mountain Ridge led throughout the game and pulled out a 72-60 win to keep its record unbeaten.

After the game was over, Mrs. Boyd peered up at Chase. "Despite what has happened, my husband would like you to join us for a welcome party tomorrow night. You can bring Allison along also." She grabbed Clementine's hand, and she stomped down the stairs.

Once she was gone, Allison glanced at Chase. "A little animosity there."

"Yeah, it's something I've gotten used to, and is just one of the reasons I can't be involved with women because they'll have to endure people like that."

She kissed him on the cheek. "If the woman loves you, she can handle anything."

They were at the bottom of the stairs when Xavier joined them. "Thanks for coming to our game, Boss. I hope you enjoyed it."

"You guys have a good team, but I will admit you're too predictable."

Xavier laughed. "What do you mean?"

"You very rarely drive to your left. A good coach will figure that out, and you'll be stopped dead in your tracks until you learn to move to your left."

"I'll remember that. Well, I should get going. The team is having an after-game party at the coach's house. We usually have plenty of pizza, which I enjoy. Again, thanks for watching us."

Chase and Allison strolled out to the parking lot to the Jeep. Chase opened the door, helped her into the vehicle, then closed the door. He slipped into the driver's seat. "Did you enjoy yourself?"

"I did," Allison said, sliding closer to Chase. "How about a movie and popcorn tonight?"

He grimaced. "I only have three channels and no DVD player."

She gasped. "Okay, then we'll play a game of cards."

The two decided to play rummy. Chase was dealing the cards when he asked Allison a question. "You don't say much about your parents."

As she picked up her cards, she explained. "My mom died when I was five, and my dad did his best to raise me and my sister, but he had a drug problem. When I turned sixteen, I left home. I haven't spoken to him in ten years."

"Have you ever thought about him?"

She drew a card. "No, I haven't. I've talked to my sister a couple of times, the last time six months ago when I first thought about leaving Willis. Haley's married to Garrett, has two children, and says she has a good life. I'm happy for her."

"You've thought about leaving Willis once before. Why didn't you?"

Allison peered at Chase. "I have no place to go."

She picked up a card, laid down her cards, and won the game.

"How about we play a game I can win?" He grinned, stood up, and held out his hand. "I know something I can win hands down."

Allison sighed. "Not tonight."

After they told each other good night, Chase sat on the

side of his bed and called his sister, Samantha. She answered after the second ring.

"What's up, Chase? I haven't heard from you in a couple of weeks. Is everything okay?"

"It is. The bookstore is still rolling. The grand reopening of the antique store was earlier this week, and it went well. I've also started a taxi service to bring older folks to the antique store and bookstore who can't get out of their homes."

"That's a wonderful idea. Has it worked?"

"It has. Those I bring here never go home without buying something. That's a good thing. How are the nieces and nephews?"

"They're all doing well. Mom and Dad are actually throwing a Valentine's Day party for the kids this weekend, something they've never done before. Gracie can't wait because she gets to play with her classmates here in the house."

"What's gotten into our parents?"

Samantha laughed. "Who knows? Are they having any kind of Valentine's Day party in Montana?"

"Yeah, they do have a Valentine's Day dinner and dance at the Shepherds' house. It should be quite the occasion—pretty much like Mom and Dad's, but just a smaller group of people."

"Do you have a date?"

Chase didn't respond right away. "No, but there is a woman here I'm interested in. Problem is she's tied into the Shepherd family, so it makes it difficult."

"What do you mean?"

"Allison is dating Willis, the lone son of the family, but the other night he beat her up, so now she's trying to figure a way out of the situation. She's afraid of the family, and I don't blame her one bit. They are powerful here and pretty much run the county, including law enforcement."

Samantha took a deep breath. "It shouldn't surprise me.

Part of the reason you called me is to help her out."

Chase laughed. "You know me so well. Yeah, I do want to help her out. The Valentine's Day party is on Saturday, so I was wondering if you could get the Connor jet out here by early Sunday morning. I'll have her ready to fly her to California, so she has a chance to think about where she's going with her life without all the pressure."

"Do you care that much about her?"

There was silence on Chase's end. "I do, but that's not the reason I'm asking you to do this for her. I'm afraid Willis or his father will do something to harm her, and I won't be able to stop it."

"You realize that when they find out what you've done, they'll come after you."

"I can handle that part of it, but I just want her to have a chance to sort things out and see what her life could become."

"I'll have the Connor jet at the Kalispell Airport early Sunday morning. Little brother, I'll make sure nothing happens to her."

Chapter 12

Sheriff Portal drained his glass of wine.

"Don't drink it so fast," Chase said, walking over to him. "You'll pass out, and someone will have to drive you home. Most likely me."

Allison joined them with two glasses of wine. "Here you go, Chase."

"Thanks."

Allison turned to the sheriff. "It is Valentine's Day, so grab your wife and enjoy the evening."

He eyeballed her. "Do you think your outfit is appropriate? What would Willis say?"

She laughed. "I haven't seen Willis in a while, but I'm sure he'll approve of it when he does." She laughed once more when the sheriff turned beet red. "You really need to get over your grumpiness."

They all turned to Willis's voice. "You look astonishing, Allison," he said, walking over to her. He kissed her on the forehead. "Happy Valentine's Day." He handed her a rose.

"Thanks, Willis. This is beautiful."

"Would you like to dance with me?"

Allison took a quick peek over at Chase and the sadness in his eyes. She turned back to Willis. "I can't, because we have so many things we need to work out."

He grabbed her arm and dragged her away from the

others. "Please let go of me. You're hurting me."

"Is it true that you're sleeping with Chase Connor?"

"I never did anything like that," she lied. "Now let me go."

Willis narrowed his eyes. "No one leaves a Shepherd, and I'm not about to let you go for anyone. If I can't have you, no one will."

Allison's eyes widened. "Please leave me alone. Get away from me." She tried to break away, but he grabbed her once more.

Chase and the sheriff hurried over. "Take your hands off her, Willis," the sheriff said.

"Who the hell do you think you are, Sheriff, to tell me what I can and can't do?"

"Willis, that's enough." Everyone turned to Nathan Shepherd's voice. "Sheriff, pardon my son's disrespect of your position."

"Dad, this isn't your concern. It's between Allison and myself."

Nathan glared at his son. "It became my issue when you disrupted our Valentine's Day activities." He turned to Allison. "I'm sorry for the way my son has handled this situation." He turned to Chase. "It seems like you've had a fairly good rapport with her the last few days. Maybe you should take her to your bookstore."

Chase stared at Nathan. "I would, but Willis already believes there's something going on between us."

"Is there?" Nathan asked.

"Nothing other than she's the bookstore manager."

Willis's mouth dropped. "I didn't know that."

Allison took a deep breath. "You didn't ask. You just assumed."

Nathan turned toward his son. "I don't see any reason for Chase not to take her to the bookstore. You two can talk tomorrow morning and sort this all out."

Chase took Allison's arm, and they walked out of the

Shepherds' house. He drove her back to the bookstore without saying a word. Once they arrived, the two climbed the stairs to the apartment.

"Thank you," she said. "I'm going to pack a bag and get out of Mountain Ridge. I can't deal with Willis or his father anymore."

Chase took her hand and walked her to the couch. "Please sit down. Do you want something to drink?"

"A beer would be wonderful right now."

He smiled. "Two beers coming up."

"What will you drink?"

They both laughed. Chase went to the refrigerator and pulled out two beers. He opened the bottles, handed one to her, and sat down next to her.

"Thanks, I need this." She took a long drink of her beer, then set it between her legs.

"I'm sorry about what happened and what was said tonight. It's all my fault this is happening. I've put you in danger, and I hope that someday you'll forgive me."

He set his beer down, took hers, put it on the table next to the couch, and wrapped his arms around her. "You can't blame yourself because the man you're dating turned out to be an abuser and control freak. It happens, but you're trying to get away from him."

"How? I have nowhere to go."

He turned her head to him. "I have a way for you to escape this nightmare, but you'll have to trust me."

Her eyes widened. "How?"

"I talked to my sister, Samantha, earlier, and she's sending the Connors' corporate jet to pick you up early tomorrow morning. I had hoped that Willis's father would step in during the celebration in his home to calm Willis down long enough for you to get out of the house. If that happened, I also believed Willis would be over here first thing in the morning to try to get you back."

"I don't know anyone in your family. Why would you

do this for me?"

Chase sighed. "Come on, you know I love you. I just wanted to give you a chance to figure out where you want to go in life, and you don't have that opportunity here because of the Shepherds. In California you will. Most importantly, no one will touch you because Samantha will make sure of that."

She kissed him. "I'm sorry I've been distant the last few days, but Willis has stressed me out. Please realize I love you despite what has happened. I know you want to spend the night with me in bed, but I'm just not ready yet. Chase, I hope you'll not hate me for it."

He gently kissed her. "Of course not, and I'll always be here for you no matter what the situation. I'll do anything I can to protect you and help you." He sipped on his beer. "One other thing, I'll need your cell phone."

She handed it to him without question. He took the little chip out of it and smashed it with his foot. "There. No one can trace you."

She gasped, then seemed to understand. Allison touched his face. "What about you? The Shepherds won't be too happy."

"Don't worry about me. I'll check on you when I come to Gracie's thirteenth birthday party next weekend. That will give you time to clear your head, take in some sun, and figure out a plan that will benefit you."

"I don't know what to say."

He touched her hands. "Just say you will?"

She smiled. "I will only if you promise to come and get me in a week."

"I promise."

She peered into his eyes, then took a deep breath. "I should go pack."

Chapter 13

"The sun isn't even up," Allison said, wiping the sleep out of her eyes. "It's only five-thirty in the morning."

Chase carried her bag toward a private airstrip near Kalispell. "It shouldn't bother you getting up so early because you slept soundly all night."

She smiled. "I should hope so, since you held me all night. Why did you do that anyway?"

"You're the one who came and slipped in next to me when I was sleeping. I'm glad you were comfortable."

They watched as a private jet coasted down the runway toward them. Ten minutes later it stopped and the ladder went down. A tall man with a suit and tie, earpiece, and shades stepped out. "Who's he?" Allison whispered.

"Samantha's security guard."

Out stepped little Gracie, who dashed toward Chase. "Uncle Chase, I got to come along to see you. Race decided to stay with Grandpa and Grandma."

Chase picked up the young girl with brown braids and hugged her.

A voice came from behind her. "Gracie, how many times have I told you not to dash down the stairs of the jet."

"Sorry, Mom, but I saw Chase and that was it."

Samantha reached over and hugged her little brother. "It's good to see you, Chase. This must be Allison?"

"Yes, ma'am," Allison said, curtsying.

Samantha grinned. "We're not that formal. Chase has told me a little bit about you."

Allison turned to Chase. "I hope nothing too embarrassing."

Samantha laughed. "No, Chase would never do that. Renaldo, our pilot, said he'd have the plane ready to go in ten minutes, so we can load your stuff on the plane, and you can say your goodbyes."

Chase carried Gracie onto the jet while Allison took her bag.

"I can tell that your daughter loves his uncle," Allison said.

"He does," Samantha said. "She has since the first time she saw him. My husband couldn't make it to her birth, so Chase was there. He was there for both of our children."

Chase stopped and turned to the two. Gracie grinned. "We can hear everything you two are saying."

Samantha reached over and tickled her. "I hope so since we're right behind you."

~

When they climbed into the jet, Allison surveyed the inside. There were several comfortable chairs, a couch, and a round table in the middle with drinks on them.

"Wow, so this is what it's like to be rich."

Gracie frowned. "You date my uncle, and you've never been inside a luxury jet?"

"Grace Amanda Brown, you apologize right now!"

Gracie hunched her shoulders when she looked at her mother. She then turned to Allison. "I'm sorry."

Allison got down on one knee so she was eye-to-eye with Gracie. "It's okay, but your uncle and I are not dating. Chase lives in an apartment upstairs from a bookstore, so I would have never seen anything luxurious with him."

Gracie stared at her mother. Samantha nodded. "Sweetheart, Uncle Chase is trying to find his own way, and it doesn't necessarily mean he'll want all the luxuries you have, but that doesn't give you the right to look down on anyone that doesn't have those luxuries."

"I'm sorry, Mom."

Allison touched Samantha's arm. "Can I talk to Chase for a moment?"

Samantha nodded. "We'll get your things and put them in storage." Once she left, Allison turned to Chase. She was getting ready to say something when she noticed the security guard watching them. "He gives me the creeps."

Chase grinned. "Get used to it. Thor will never let you out of his sight for the next week. The only time you'll have any peace is in your room."

"Why?"

Chase took a deep breath. "It's a normal procedure for the Connors. He's been assigned to protect you."

Allison sighed. "He's Samantha's security guard. Besides, no one watches over you."

"He is and he isn't Samantha's security guard. When Samantha goes out on the town or with friends or shopping, then he's with her. Otherwise, he's assigned to those at the manor, and since you'll be there, he's the one who will be watching over you. Thor is quiet, unassuming, but no one will touch you."

She sighed. "I don't know what to say about all of this other than I want to thank you for what you've done. I will miss your laugh, your corny jokes, and watching you stack those books on shelves." They both laughed. She wrapped her arms around his neck. "But most of all, I'll miss you." She reached up and kissed him solidly on the lips. Once she regained her breath, she said to him, "Don't forget to come and get me next weekend. You promised."

"I promise."

Thor joined them. "Sorry, Master Chase, but the jet is ready to leave. Ms. Allison, please join the others and buckle in. I'll make sure nothing happens to her."

"You do that, Thor."

Allison watched as Chase left the jet. Once he was gone, the door closed, and the jet headed down the runway. Samantha sat in a chair next to Allison. "Don't worry, you'll see him again."

"I hope so."

"I don't understand," Samantha said.

Allison turned to face Chase's sister. "I don't know if the Shepherds will ever forgive him."

She patted Allison's leg. "Don't you dare worry about Chase. You two will be walking down the aisle one of these days."

Allison laughed. "Why would you think that?"

Samantha wrapped her arm around Allison. "I'm in love with my husband, and I see some of the same looks you give Chase—the same eyes that glisten when he's around, and if I'm not mistaken, you have that same lump in your throat whenever he's gone."

"I may have blown that chance over the last week."

Hours later, Allison opened her eyes to a pair of dark eyes staring at her.

"You decided to wake up. We're about ready to land in San Diego, and you slept for a long while. You must not be used to getting up so early."

She smiled at Gracie. "I'm not. I've never been to San Diego. Is it as pretty as everyone says?"

Gracie nodded. "I love it here because the sun's always shining. It's a good thing Mom brought coats along when we came to Montana, or we would have frozen to death running off the jet."

"It does get cold." Allison turned to the little girl. "You should probably buckle up because it seems like we're going to be landing."

Gracie jumped into the seat next to her and put on the belt without question. Allison smiled at her. She smiled back. "My Uncle Chase trusts you, so I can sit by you."

"I won't let anything happen to you."

They both looked out the window as they descended from the sky. Allison's eyes went wide. "It's like we're landing in the Pacific Ocean."

Gracie giggled. "The first time that happened with Uncle Chase and me, I had to crawl into his lap because I was so scared. You can sit on my lap if you're scared."

Allison smiled. "Thanks for the offer, but I think I'll be just fine here."

The jet landed in a private landing strip, and the group walked off with their bags. Allison noticed that Thor stuck close to her as they headed to a limousine waiting for them.

A short man with half a mustache held the door open for them. "Ms. Samantha, I hope your flight was enjoyable."

"Like always, Walter. This is Ms. Allison, who is very special to Chase."

"Ah," Walter said. "Ms. Allison, it's wonderful to meet you. Anyone who is special to Master Chase will be well taken care of."

Once they were in the limousine, Allison whispered to Samantha, "What's this all about?"

She smiled at Allison. "Now everyone knows who you are."

"I don't understand."

"Everyone respects my little brother and will do anything for him, so now that they know you're important to him, they'll do the same for you."

"I don't want this."

Samantha sighed. "None of us do."

Chapter 14

All morning Chase had been yawning. He laughed to himself knowing that Allison was right; they had gotten up way too early. Allison had texted him that they had arrived in San Diego. He wouldn't bother her until later so she had a chance to catch her breath.

Throughout the morning, several people had come in the bookstore to browse the shelves. It was close to noon when Nathan walked through the door. "Mr. Shepherd, what can I do for you? Are you interested in any books?"

Nathan unbuttoned his coat and peered around the bookstore. "I will say that you've done a good job sprucing up the bookstore, but then of course being a Connor, you do have the money to do most anything you want. That includes stealing my son's lovely girlfriend from him."

Chase frowned. "What do you want?"

"You're a Connor, always right to the point. We both know that you and Allison have something going on together. I'm sure that you spent many nights with her, but that's not why I'm here. I could care less. What I do care about is how you can help me with a resort that is being proposed in the area."

Chase shook his head, a smirk erupting. "I know nothing about a resort, and even if I did, I wouldn't be part of it, especially if a Shepherd was involved."

"Now now, Why would you feel like that?"

Chase peered into the older man's eyes. "I want nothing to do with a man who allows his son to beat a woman because he didn't get his way. The chestnut doesn't fall far from the tree, so it makes me wonder if he's learned about abusing women from his father."

Nathan frowned at Chase. "Is Allison here?"

"When I woke up, she was gone, her bags included."

"You wouldn't happen to know where she went?"

Chase shrugged. "That's her business, not mine."

Nathan laughed. "I can see we're not going to get along too well. We'll find her." He spun on his heels.

"What's so important about finding Allison?"

Nathan turned and glared at Chase. "No one leaves a Shepherd."

~

Allison gawked at the Connor house, a mansion on top of a hill that looked out on the Pacific Ocean for miles and miles. They pulled up to the front of a house that was bigger than any she had ever seen. Walter opened the door of the limousine, and they all stepped out.

Allison's mouth hung open at how large the mansion was. It had more glass than she had ever seen in a building other than an office complex. Once inside, she stepped into an open living space.

Gracie took her hand and led her toward a large window that overlooked the Pacific Ocean.

"This is amazing," Allison said.

"It's one of our three living rooms, the smallest of the three," Samantha said standing beside them. "The Pacific Ocean is just the icing on the cake."

Allison turned to Samantha. "How big is this place?"

"It's close to six thousand square feet in the house, but there are several gathering spaces in addition to the main house, including a place where we hold all of our social functions. It's larger than a football field. The house itself has seven bedrooms and six bathrooms, plus three living room spaces, which allows us to offer three different social events at any given time."

A young woman joined them. "Ms. Samantha, the room is ready."

"Thank you, Maya." Samantha turned to Allison. "This is Maya, one of the ladies that works here. She'll handle all your needs while you're here."

"Needs?" Allison asked.

Samantha smiled. "If you need anything, she'll get it for you. That will include any type of food or drink. She'll make sure your room is clean, prepare a bath—anything you need, just ask her."

Allison was incredulous. "Chase lived like this?"

Samantha laughed. "No, he was a bit different. He took care of things on his own, but he asked that I take care of you, and I will."

"He did?"

"He sure did."

They all turned at a lady hurrying in. Her hair was short and brown, her makeup was caked on her face, and she wore a blue, strapless dress with heels. "Is this the guest of the house?"

Samantha smiled. "Mom, this is Allison Winters."

The lady pulled her into a hug. "It's wonderful to meet you. My name is Tricia, and as you've heard, Samantha is my daughter. You'll meet the rest of the family this afternoon at the social."

Allison leaned toward Samantha and whispered, "I don't have any clothes for anything like that."

"Don't worry. It's all taken care of."

Tricia interrupted. "I hope you enjoy your stay here. If you need anything, please ask Maya and it will be taken care of."

Once Tricia left, Samantha took her elbow. "Let's show you where you're staying while you're here."

Samantha and Allison climbed up twenty stairs to the

second floor, then walked down a corridor, and at the end of it, Samantha opened up a door. "This is Chase's room, and it's where you'll be staying as long as you like. I'll give you some time to take all of this in, and in an hour, Maya will come and get you so we can do some shopping."

Allison lifted her head. "I have no money."

Samantha smiled. "Chase took care of that. He wanted me to give this to you once you were settled."

Samantha handed her an envelope, turned, and left the room.

Allison tossed the envelope on the king-sized bed and gazed at the photos on the wall of Chase when he was younger. She leaned close to study a photo of him when he was about thirteen. Chase already had that gorgeous smile.

A knock at the door brought her back to the present. "Come in."

The door opened and Maya stepped in. "Ms. Allison, here is a cell phone for you to use while you're here. Ms. Samantha told me to tell you that the charges are covered, and when you make calls, they won't be traced back to you." She handed Allison the phone.

"Thank you, Maya. Please just call me Allison."

Maya smiled. "Allison, it is. Also, Mr. Thor is always outside your room so you will be safe."

Allison peeked out the door and waved her fingers at Thor. He waved back. She peered back at Maya. "Does he ever smile?"

"Very rarely."

Maya left, closing the door behind her. She sat down on the bed to open the envelope. "Money." She started counting and finished with five thousand dollars in cash. "What were you thinking, Chase?" she whispered. She put the money back in the envelope, placed it in a drawer, and stepped outside onto the terrace where two chairs sat overlooking the Pacific Ocean. What a view!

Allison kicked off her shoes and sat on the lounge chair.

She peered at the time on the cell phone. Eleven, meaning it would be noon in Montana. She dialed Chase's cell phone, and he answered after a couple of rings.

"Is it lunchtime?" she asked him when he picked up.

"As a matter of fact, I'm getting ready to make myself a peanut butter and jelly sandwich."

"Wow, that sounds like a joyful meal. I don't know what they have planned for lunch for me here. We're going shopping after lunch, so I have clothes for a social event this afternoon."

"That sounds like my parents. They do that for any guests they have. Then tomorrow night you'll get to meet all of the bigwigs they deal with."

Allison sighed. "Why did you give me five thousand dollars?"

Chase had finished chewing part of his sandwich. "You'll need money to do things you want to do there, like purchasing some clothes. Consider it an advance on your salary."

Allison took a deep breath. "I don't want this, Chase. This is way too much for me. I'm just a simple girl not meant to be with a rich guy. Willis has nothing compared to what you have here."

"No one is asking you to be a rich girl. Just relax and enjoy being pampered for a week, because it'll give you a chance to unwind and figure out where you want to go with your life. There's nothing wrong with someone taking care of you for once like you've taken care of others."

"You know about me helping the senior citizens, but this is much different. Hold it, did someone tell you I help at the shelter?"

"I've been told several times people who live in Mountain Ridge know everything that is happening with everyone else."

Allison sighed. "Jake. Damn, he has a big mouth."

Chase laughed. "No, it was actually Milo who told me

about you working at the shelter, and I think that's really cool that you do that."

Allison changed the subject. "Are you still coming on Friday? I miss you terribly."

"I promised I'll be there, and I will."

Allison sipped on her drink. "What about the Shepherds? Are they causing you problems?"

"You promised you would only think about yourself while you were in California."

"I did, but I still worry about what they could do to you."

Chase sighed. "They won't do anything to me because they need me to help with this crazy resort they're talking about. At least that's what Nathan is talking about."

"You think it's more?"

"Again, stop worrying about it and enjoy yourself."

"I can't because I love you, and I don't want anything to happen to you." When Chase didn't respond, Allison did, "I'm sorry. I shouldn't have said that."

"No, it's okay, you just kind of took me by surprise. I should get off the phone here. Please relax and enjoy yourself."

Once they were disconnected, Allison took a deep breath. She'd scared him away, and that wasn't what she wanted. Once she arrived in California, she knew exactly that she wanted Chase in her life, but then she'd known that all along.

Chapter 15

Allison and Samantha spent the afternoon shopping for outfits, souvenirs, and other things that she would bring back to Montana with her, and yes, Allison would go back to Montana. Many times, photographers tried to take photos of them, but Thor stopped them by grabbing their cameras or phones and smashing them with his foot. When that happened, Samantha followed up by handing them a gift card to buy a new one.

Allison was amazed at the paparazzi that hovered nearby. She turned to Samantha. "How do you deal with this all the time?"

She had just bought a smoothie and was sipping it. "We've been hounded since before we were Gracie's age, so it becomes natural. I try to keep the kids away from them as much as possible, but at times it doesn't work. The reason Thor is destroying their devices is because Chase asked that I make sure that no photos were ever taken of you, so they wouldn't get back to the Shepherds. Of course, it's always difficult to make sure we get them all, but Thor is pretty thorough and can spot cameras from unique places. I have no idea how he does it."

Allison sipped on her iced tea. "What is Thor's real name? Or is it just Thor?"

Samantha smiled. "His real name is Bryant Elias Thorson, but everyone knows him as Thor. He came to the family right after Gracie was born. Chase hired him because he saw something in him that my family didn't. The parents put up a stink, but Chase stuck to his guns and paid him out of his inheritance, and he's been watching over my children and me ever since."

After another hour of shopping, they headed back to the mansion arriving around four-thirty. Maya was carrying plates and glasses for the party when they walked in.

"Ms. Samantha, guests will be arriving in an hour and your mother said there'll be more people than expected."

"There will?" Samantha asked, confused.

Maya smiled. "They've been told that Mr. Chase has a new girlfriend, and everyone wants to see her."

Allison frowned. "I told Chase earlier I don't want to be a burden."

Samantha laughed. "You don't know my parents. Just try to have fun, be yourself, and don't be surprised if you get hit on by several eligible, handsome, rich bachelors."

"What do you mean?" Allison asked.

Samantha wrapped her arm around Allison. "Men and women alike come to these parties to pick up the opposite sex for the evening. The next morning it's all forgotten, and they move on with their lives."

"Even if they're married?"

Samantha nodded. "Even if they're married."

Allison walked up the stairs into the bedroom, and lay down on the bed. She thought to herself, "what a nice, soft bed." She could cuddle and fall asleep. Then she thought about what Samantha said about being picked up. She didn't want that, but she wouldn't be rude either and not attend the party.

It was after five-thirty when Maya had finished helping her do her hair, her makeup, and fix her dress. "There, you're going to be the belle of the ball."

Allison smiled. "Thanks for all of your help. You do a very good job."

Maya blushed. "Thank you, that's the first time anyone has ever said that to me."

Allison didn't know what to say so she changed the subject. "Could you take a photo of me so I could send it to Chase?"

"Sure, I will." Maya stepped back and snapped a few pictures of her in her new strapped, long blue dress, with platform ankle boots. Allison primped and smiled, fluffing her blonde curls and batting her sparkling blue eyes.

After Maya handed Allison the cell phone, she viewed the photos, and sent three of them to Chase. A few moments later a message dinged. *You may be the most beautiful woman in the world.*

Maya must have noticed her blushing. "He must have said something nice."

"He did," Allison said, then took a deep breath. "I'm ready for this even though I don't want to be here."

Maya laughed. "No one likes these parties except drunks and oversexed guests." Maya covered her mouth quickly. "I'm sorry I should have never said that. Please don't say anything."

Allison touched Maya. "Don't worry, I'll never say anything that you or I talk about."

"Thank you."

Samantha introduced Allison to many of her friends throughout the evening. They were talking when a man with white hair and glasses joined them.

"I finally get to meet a rare beauty at these boring events."

Samantha took the man's arm. "Okay, Dad, quit embarrassing the lady."

Allison blushed. "Mr. Connor, it's so nice to meet you."

He smiled. "And you too, young lady. Chase hasn't mentioned you at all in his conversations with us, but then he doesn't say much about anyone. Even when he was a child, he kept to himself."

"That's one of the traits I enjoy about Chase because I know I can say anything, and it will never be repeated. Unlike so many others."

Oliver Connor laughed. "Are you saying I'm like those others?"

Allison's hand went to her lips. "I don't know you that well, so I can't answer that question fairly."

"Chase has a winner here."

Allison shook her head. "You have the wrong idea, sir. Chase and I are not together. I wish everyone would quit saying that because Chase and I are friends, that's all."

Oliver grinned. "If you say so." He turned to a voice. "It was nice meeting you. Well, there are others here I need to greet." He winked at Allison as he left.

"He was quite nice," Allison said.

"Yeah, you've caught him on one of his rare, nice occasions. Usually, he's digging for information to help increase our portfolio."

"Then I'm safe because there's nothing I can provide him. Your brothers are attorneys, but what do you do?"

Samantha tasted her Champagne. "I'm an attorney also. We are all attorneys and we've been so for over a hundred years. You realize that Chase is the richest of any of the Connors?"

Allison shook her head. "Chase and I have never talked about money, but I do know he doesn't care about it; he just cares about his bookstore and antique store. He's done a great job renovating the old building and has hired wonderful help to keep it going."

"How does he keep it going?"

The ladies turned to an older guy who looked like Chase, but more refined with a cropped beard and a perfect haircut. Samantha introduced him to Allison. "This is our brother, Micah."

"Nice to meet you," Allison said. Micah took her hand and kissed it. "The others are right; you are one beautiful woman. If I wasn't married, I'd be sure to make a play for you."

Allison frowned. "It would never happen. I just broke up with a guy who thinks he's better than others and can be a pompous ass."

Samantha and Micah laughed. "You know me well," Micah said. "Anyway, back to an explanation on how Chase is making it work."

"He does little things like giving older people rides so they can come in and browse, or helping them order books from other places, or even driving to different locations to pick up antiques to add to the collection. Recently, he drove to Helena in a blizzard to pick up a chest full of antique dresses, which sold out immediately."

"In a blizzard? Why would he do something crazy like that?" Samantha asked.

Allison shrugged. "It didn't start out as a blizzard, but it ended up that way, and we slid down into Missoula."

"We?" Micah asked.

"Yeah, I was stupid enough to ride along with him, but I had an enjoyable time, and before you get any ideas, nothing happened between the two of us. I'm merely the manager of the bookstore."

"At least for now." Micah smiled.

Allison tasted her wine. "I'm not really interested in a guy right now. I've had enough of socializing and just want a breather."

Samantha pointed to a gate. "You can walk down to the ocean and enjoy its beauty."

"Thanks. I think I'll do that right now."

Once through the gate, she took off her ankle boots and carried them. She stopped and turned to Thor, who was standing there. "I'll be right down there, sitting on the sand with my feet in the ocean."

Thor smiled. "I'll be watching you."

She smiled back at her. "You do smile."

Chapter 16

Once Allison had reached the beach, she sat down in the sand and placed her feet in the water, feeling the waves rush through her toes. Chase was right, despite the crowd in the family mansion, this was what she needed to straighten out her head.

She was excited when she saw what looked like a whale lift up out of the water a distance from her. Allison had already started to think about where her life was taking her. It wouldn't be with Willis Shepherd, but she was still worried that something would happen to Chase because of her.

She took a deep breath, feeling the water crash against her feet, and taking in the sounds of the ocean. Allison loved the mountains at night, but this was just as magnificent. Her head lifted at the sound of a female voice.

"I didn't mean to scare you." a lady approached who looked just a bit older than her. "Do you mind if I join you?"

"Please do. I'm Allison."

The brown-haired lady smiled. "I know. I'm Olivia, Micah's wife. It seems like I'm like you. I needed a breath of fresh air from the party. It gets tiring after a while going to all of these shindigs that are put on by the Connors and others."

"I can imagine it would be tough being a Connor."

Olivia nodded. "I love Micah, but you're right, I don't

enjoy all of this, and I sure don't like the way he hits on women and they him."

Allison's eyes widened. "Why do you put up with it?"

She sighed. "To be truthful, I just found out about it recently. I've been married to Micah for five years, and we have two children. How naive I was. To answer your question, Micah loves me in his own way. And more importantly, this family protects those who belong to it, which is vital for my children." Olivia pulled her hair into a messy bun. "I'm sure you've found that out in after one afternoon with Samantha—all the cameras that flash their way. What you haven't seen are all the perverts who are looking to take our children for money. That guy standing up by the gate is the best security guard in the family. It's like he knows what's going to happen before it happens."

"I've noticed that, but he did actually smile."

Olivia laughed. "That has to be a first. I don't know if anyone's seen the guy smile, but then all ten of the security guards are like that."

"Why do they need ten?"

"One for Oliver, one for Tricia, and one for each of the kids, which brings that to seven, then there are three others that monitor the Connor mansion, which includes ten acres along the ocean."

"I've never seen a house this big."

Olivia laughed. "It's one of the smaller ones in this area." She stood up. "I probably should get back to the crowd."

Allison jumped up also. "I'll join you."

Once back in the mansion, Allison and Olivia found Samantha who was with another guy that wasn't her husband, Steven. Olivia joined Micah who was talking to another guy, so Allison decided to grab some food at the buffet table. She remembered the security guard and joined him outside.

"Would you like something to eat, Thor?"

He shook his head. "I'll eat later, ma'am."

She stood by him. "Are you always this uptight?"

He smiled once more. "These ties do it to me all the time. I wished Chase would be in charge because he would ban ties."

Allison laughed. "I can imagine he would. I'm grabbing something to eat. Are you sure you don't want anything?"

Thor shook his head.

"Your loss."

After Allison grabbed a plateful of food, she noticed Samantha was standing by herself. She strolled toward her.

Samantha smiled at her. "I see you found the buffet."

"I was getting hungry, so I grabbed some riblets, salad, and wine to wash them down."

"The riblets are usually pretty good," Samantha said.

"I'll let you know right now." She tasted her riblet. "Very good. Do you want one?"

Samantha smiled. "I'll grab something later."

A couple of hours later, as everyone was starting to leave, Allison stood at the gate with a glass of wine staring at the ocean.

"Is everything okay?"

She turned to Micah who had walked up to her. "I'm just wondering how I got myself into this mess—being involved with Willis Shepherd and his family. What a bonehead!"

Micah stood next to her. "Do you want to talk about it?"

She lifted her head to him. "I don't know you that well at all, so never mind. I am tired, so I'm heading to bed."

"Good night."

It was eleven when Allison opened her bedroom door. She stripped down and slipped into one of two nightgowns she had purchased earlier that day. Once finished, she climbed into bed and was fast asleep the moment she hit her pillow.

Her eyes popped open the next morning when the cell

phone rang. She clawed for the phone and finally grabbed it after the third ring. It was six in the morning. In a groggy voice, she said, "Good morning."

"Get out of bed and enjoy the California sunshine and Pacific Ocean."

"Chase, it's seven in the morning in Montana. What are you doing up this early?"

He sighed. "You've been gone only two days, and you don't even remember that I get up early every morning?"

She giggled. "You're right, but I do believe I had a little too much wine last night, and I'm feeling it this morning."

"Oh my, you're already becoming a member of the Connor family."

Allison groaned. "Don't you dare say that. I saw and heard enough last night to tell me to stay as far away as possible from the Connors and those they hang out with."

Chase laughed. "That bad, huh?"

"I don't have enough fingers and toes to count the number of times guys hit on me. I even had two gals try to connect with me."

"That's what you get for being the most beautiful gal at the ball."

She was quiet. "Do you believe I was beautiful last night?"

She could tell he was drinking coffee. "If I was there, we may have wound up in my bed at the end of the evening."

She giggled. "That would have been the highlight of my evening. But of course, when you show up at the end of the week, maybe we can do that anyway. Are you still coming?"

"I am. That is, if I don't get stuck in another blasted blizzard. They're talking about a major snowstorm coming through the area starting on Friday night into the weekend. Will it ever stop snowing here?"

"In June and July. Why did you call me so early?"

He took another sip of his drink. "I just wanted to say

good morning and ask how you were doing."

Allison leaned up against the bed. "If I didn't know any better, I'd think you cared about me more than you're letting on."

"How's the bed?"

Allison laughed. "Way to dodge the question. The bed is amazingly comfortable. I want to get a bed like this, but I'm sure I can't afford it."

"If you didn't spend any of your advance pay, you'd be able to buy yourself one, but since you spent at least a couple of hundred bucks for that dress and platform shoes, that's probably out of the question."

"Now how would you know how much those cost?"

He sighed. "I have a sister and several sisters-in-law who enjoy the shopping scene. I hear all about how much the dresses, nightgowns, and shoes cost from my brothers. By the way, there should be a knock on your door right about now."

Allison turned to the knock on the door. "Just a moment." She turned back to her conversation. "How did you know?"

"Gracie promptly wakes guests and her uncle at six-thirty every morning. Enjoy your day."

Allison started to hang up. "Chase, thank you, I am enjoying myself here, especially the ocean, but I do miss you."

"It's not the same without you here either."

She was quiet for a bit. "Do you mean that?"

"I do. Now answer the door before Thor comes through thinking something happened to you."

"Would he do that?"

"In about ten seconds. Go."

Allison turned off the cell phone, jumped off the bed, and hurried over to open the door. "Good morning, Gracie."

The young girl's hands were posted on her waist. "Just in time. Thor was about ready to come through the door to make sure everything was okay."

Allison grinned. "A gal needs time to wake up out of her sleep."

Gracie smiled. "Chase did that thirty minutes ago."

Chapter 17

Allison joined the others at the breakfast table which consisted of eggs, pancakes, bacon, and waffles, along with fruit and juice. She grabbed some eggs and fruit, and orange juice, then sat at the only open seat next to a man in his forties with a beard and glasses. "Good morning, sir."

"You too, ma'am. I'm sure you're wondering who I am. I'm Keenan, Chase's oldest brother."

"Nice to meet you. You look nothing like Chase."

He grinned. "Yeah. I'm the better looking of the two."

She smiled. "You wish."

Everyone around the table laughed. Samantha jumped in. "You didn't get to meet the whole family last night. You've met our parents, my husband, Steven, Micah and his wife, Olivia. Now, Keenan. Over there on the corner are Arthur and his wife, Sylvia. Across from you are Roderick, and his wife, Beth."

"Nice to meet you all. No wife, Keenan?"

He grinned. "I do have a girlfriend. You'll meet Dolly this evening."

Tricia jumped in. "I'm in charge of your entertainment for the day."

"You don't have to do that, Mrs. Connor. I can keep myself occupied around here."

Oliver jumped in. "Nonsense, young lady. You're our guest, and we'll make sure you enjoy yourself."

"Or never want to come back," Micah said with a grin.

Allison grinned. "I see you make smart-alecky comments just like Chase."

"Where do you think he got it from?"

Tricia interrupted. "It's settled. You're with me."

Roderick tapped Allison's hand. "You don't say no to our mother."

Throughout the day Allison and Tricia toured different sites around the area including Coronado Bay, the San Diego Zoo, and took an hour-long cruise around the San Diego Bay.

As they stood on the deck, Tricia glanced at Allison. "What are you and Chase?"

"What do you mean?"

"Are you dating? Are you sleeping together, an employee with benefits? What are you?"

Allison glared at Tricia. "Wow, that's the only reason you spent time with me to find out about Chase and me? Even if there was something going on with Chase and me, after that comment I would never tell you a thing."

Tricia narrowed her eyes. "You're a sassy young lady."

"I'm not. It's just that I dated a guy whose family was controlling, and that's why I ended up here this week. I needed to get away. I will tell you that Chase and I are not an item, and we most likely won't ever be."

"Why?"

"Like I said, I was involved with a guy who had a controlling father, and I see some of the same tendencies with you and your husband. There is no way I'll go through that again."

Tricia grinned. "No wonder Chase likes you."

Allison's eyes widened. "Why would you even suggest something like that?"

"Just a feeling I have, but that doesn't matter right now. You need to know that Chase doesn't allow his parents or family to control his life, so if you two ever get together, that will never be a concern for you. No one was for him moving to Montana. They want him to take over the family law firm."

"Why him? He's the youngest of the family."

"He's also the brightest and the richest."

Allison finished the chocolate bar she had purchased. "I've seen his intelligence, but rich? I would have never sensed that."

Tricia studied Allison. "You have no idea who Chase Connor is, do you?"

"I know what I need to know. He's kind, he's smart, and he cares about people."

She chuckled. "Not many gals talk about my boys like that. Most do mention they're good looks, but I sense it's because they have all this money, and people know it in California."

"Mrs. Connor, Chase and I have never talked about money. In fact, the thing we talk about most is what he wants to do with his life. He wants to make sure the bookstore and antique store are the best they can be. Chase never talks about marriage or dating gals."

"That's strange because Chase is the one guy every gal is after, including my daughters-in-law, but then he has always been different. The point I'm trying to make is that the family wants Chase to take over the law firm because they know he's innovative, and it sounds like he's using his creative skills with the two businesses in Montana." She sipped her drink. "Our family is worth more than $55 billion, and Chase has more than $30 billion of that money, so as you can see, he can do anything he wants. Why he hasn't said anything to you about his money, I can't answer that."

Allison sighed. "Simple, money doesn't matter to him. The boat is at the dock. Guess we should get back."

Once they'd returned to the mansion, Allison said, "I had a wonderful day, Mrs. Connor. Thank you. I especially enjoyed the talk we had on the cruise ship. It was enlightening."

The next morning Allison was ready for Chase's phone call, and she answered immediately. "Ten seconds late," she giggled.

"Were you waiting for me to call?"

"You bet I was. I'm lying in your bed thinking about what's been happening. I know for sure Willis and I are through, and I want nothing to do with him or his family. After that I'm not sure."

"That's a start."

"I spent the day with your mother yesterday."

Chase's sigh came through the phone. "I'm sorry if she made it rough on you."

"Not too bad, but she did bring up some things you never mentioned to me, but then why would you? How can you be worth more than $30 billion and be in Montana running a bookstore and antique store?"

He sighed. "Money means nothing to me."

"That's exactly what I told your mother. I also found out your older brother, Keenan, thinks he's the most handsome man in the family."

"He's always said that."

"Enough about California. "Tell me, what's happening with you and the Shepherds?"

"Nothing."

"Chase Connor, don't lie to me."

"Wow, that's the first time I've ever heard your voice rise."

She sighed. "I'm sorry, it's just that I'm tired of people not answering my questions when I ask them. Don't be like others, please."

"Okay. Nathan Shepherd stopped by the day you left and accused me of stealing his son's girlfriend. He believes we have something going on, but could care less if we sleep together. Nathan just wants me to help him with this resort that's being proposed."

"What did you say?"

"I told him I wanted nothing to do with a man who allows his son to beat a woman, and since it's a learned trait, Nathan must be a wife abuser. They're looking for you."

"Will they find me?"

"Nope. You're safe in California, but once you come back, they'll know immediately."

"Who said I was coming back?"

Chase took a deep breath. "Weren't you the one who told me to promise to come and get you?"

She giggled. "Yeah, but maybe I like it enough here I'll want to stay."

"That's your choice."

Now was the time to tell him. "I need to talk to someone about what happened that night with Willis. Until I do, I'll never get rid of the feelings I have."

"Talk to Olivia."

"Not Samantha?"

"Talk to Olivia. She'll tell you her story and will never repeat anything you tell her."

"Thanks. I'm going to go now because I need to get ready for your little niece. I miss you."

"Same here."

Allison stood at the door and stared at her cell phone. At exactly seven-thirty she whipped the door open to see Gracie's goofy stare. "What took you so long?" Allison said, rubbing her head. Thor stood there smiling with Gracie. Allison winked at him, and the man blushed.

After she wrapped her arm around Gracie, Allison glanced up at Thor. "I've seen you smile and now blush. What's next?"

Chapter 18

Since it was Thursday, the Connors decided to take the day off and enjoy a cruise on the yacht with their family and few friends.

Allison's mouth stood agape as she and Samantha boarded the yacht. "Wow, how big is this?"

"More than 250 feet. Wait until you see the inside."

Allison stopped when she stepped inside to look at everything. A wraparound couch for at least a dozen people clustered with cushion chairs around a large wooden table with a glass cover. Outside were a hot tub and pool.

Olivia took her hand. "You want to see the dining area?"

The two walked into the next room. There sat a glass table that fit twenty-four people. "Amazing."

"It is. I was just as shocked as you were the first time I stepped onboard. The beds are very comfortable. On the backside of the yacht is an area just to lounge around in. That's where I usually go because everyone else prefer to lounge by the pool. Would you like to join me?"

"I would love to."

The yacht set sail out of San Diego harbor toward Coronado Bay. An hour into the trip, Allison and Olivia grabbed a couple of drinks and went to the empty lounge area. They set their drinks by two chaises lounge and lay down.

"This is beautiful," Allison said, looking out at the ocean.

"And peaceful. I adore my two kids, but I need some time to myself, and that's why the Connor family is worth it despite all the craziness involved with them. They even hired a lifeguard for the day."

Allison sipped on her glass of wine. "Chase suggested I talk to you because you went through the same thing I've gone through."

"I don't understand."

Allison drained her wine and pushed her glass toward Oliva, signaling she'd like another.

Olivia stared at her. "Wow, it must have been something big." Olivia took the bottle and poured another glass for her. "Calm down and tell me what happened."

Allison took a deep breath. "I had a boyfriend named Willis Shepherd. You may have heard of the Shepherd name."

Olivia nodded. "Micah has mentioned the Connor family working with them on a resort project in Montana. He didn't think much of them, but his father said he wanted to check into it. Then Oliver Connor said, 'Go for it.'"

"Correct. Anyway, I spent the night with Chase at a scavenger hunt where we were able to find gold coins as well as crack a case that had been hindering the sheriff's department for several years. The next afternoon I went over to Willis's house, and he wanted to have sex with me. When I refused, he forced himself on me, and I screamed because it hurt so bad. He slammed my face against the floor leaving bruises. So I ran to Chase's apartment."

"Did you tell him?"

Allison sipped her second glass of wine. "He saw the bruises, so of course I told him about that, but I didn't tell him what else happened to me."

"Did you call the cops?"

"I couldn't because Willis's father owns the county

sheriff's department. So, I didn't know what to do. That's why I'm here. Chase sent me here so I could pull myself together. I'm coming along, but I can't get over the rape. I don't know what to do, but Chase said you could help me."

Olivia sat up and took her hands. "When I was seventeen, I was out with my girlfriends and ran into a handsome guy who I wanted to be with. To make a long story short, he got rough, smacked me around, and forced himself into me also. A few weeks later I found out I was pregnant."

"What did you do?"

"I couldn't call the police either, so I lived with it for a few months until I was able to meet with a woman who helped me through it. Now, I'm as good as new, but it wasn't easy."

"Did they find the guy?"

"Yeah, he wasn't hard to find. I married him."

Allison's eyes dropped. "I don't understand."

Olivia took a deep breath. "The simple answer is I loved Micah, and I always have. I was able to forgive him for what happened, partly because we both were drunk, but also he's made it up to me in so many ways, especially being there for our two children and me. Do you love Willis?"

"Oh gosh, no. I don't know if I ever did."

"Do you love Chase?"

"I'm trying to figure that out."

Olivia sipped her drink. "A couple of things you need to do. First, find out if you're pregnant or if he did something to your insides."

"I don't have the money for that."

"You're fortunate that the Connors have the best and most discreet doctor there is. She just happens to be on the yacht today and can check you over right now if you wish."

"And second?"

"You have to tell Chase."

"How do I do that?"

Olivie sighed. "You don't have to if you don't care about him, but we both know that's not the case. The first thing is to find out what happened to you. We'll find you a room, and I'll bring her to you."

"Right here? What about the others?"

"This yacht is the best time and place because the others are too invested in what they're doing on deck. The only one who will know is whoever you choose to tell."

"You'll know."

Olivia shook her head. "I won't know the outcome. Let's go."

The two found an outside room on the yacht. Olivia disappeared, and five minutes later returned with a lady with glasses carrying a medical bag. "Allison Winters?"

Allison nodded.

"Don't be frightened. Olivia told me what happened, and we'll figure it out together. My name is Dr. Lucy Kardell, and I've been the Connors' doctor for the past ten years. Anything you say won't leave this room."

Allison frowned. "How do I know this room isn't bugged or there aren't camera devices in it?"

The doctor smiled. "You're right, the other rooms are bugged, but this one isn't because it's the room where I do my checkups when we're out on the ocean. Even Oliver Connor doesn't want his ailments broadcast around the world. We're safe here."

The doctor put her bag down. "There's a changing room right there. Please change into the garment inside, and we'll take a look at you to see what we can figure out."

Five minutes later, Allison entered the room that was equipped as well as any doctor's office she'd been in.

The doctor bade her climb on the examination chair. "Lie back down, and I'll check things out. Please tell me if anything hurts?"

Allison sighed. "It has hurt several times right near my private parts."

"Okay, we'll start there. Does this hurt?"

She winced. "Yes, it does."

"And this?"

"Not as bad."

She probed for several more minutes and then stopped. "I'm going to give you a pregnancy test just to make sure. I don't think you're pregnant, but you do have torn tissue in the entrance area that will heal in time."

Allison took the pregnancy test, and it came back negative. She took a deep breath. "That's the best news I've heard today."

Dr. Kardell stepped back and gazed at Allison. "From what I've seen, the damage seems superficial, but time will tell if there's any permanent damage."

Allison's eyes watered. "What do you mean? You mean I may not be able to have children?"

"I'm not positive, but I've seen cases like this where a man has raped a woman and caused irreparable damage. Did you call law enforcement about this?"

"I didn't because it wouldn't have done any good."

"How would you know that?"

Allison clammed up. Dr. Kardell frowned. "Right, his father owns law enforcement and the courts. I've seen it so many times, including right here with the Connors."

As she was checking Allison, Dr. Kardell continued conversing. "Okay, so you've decided to move on with your life and not press charges?"

Allison nodded. "I'm sure you don't believe that's the right thing to do."

Dr. Kardell smiled. "I don't judge. I've seen things in the last ten years that most doctors don't deal with. Whether you file charges or not you'll have to deal with the stigma associated with what has happened. The best advice I can give you is to associate yourself with those whom you trust and love."

"That may be the hardest part."

Chapter 19

"Uncle Chase, you're here."

Chase turned to see his niece, Gracie, running toward him, with Allison and Samantha following behind. Samantha held Race's hand while Thor stood near the baggage claim watching.

Chase lifted Gracie up and held her tight. "I told you I wouldn't miss your party." He set her down, then picked up Race and hugged him. Next came Samantha. He turned to Allison whose blue eyes sparkled.

They hugged. "I missed you," she said.

He kissed her. "I missed you also."

They walked out to the limo waiting for them.

The silver-mustached man opened the door for him. "Master Chase, it's good to see you again."

"Walter, you're still here?"

He grinned at Chase. "They just can't get rid of me."

They all climbed into the limousine, then headed toward the mansion on the Pacific Ocean. The limousine arrived at the Connor estate forty-five minutes later. Chase stepped out of the limo, staring at the large mansion.

Samantha grabbed his arm. "Is everything okay?"

He continued staring at the mansion. "I never realized how big this place was. Why does anyone need a house that has seven bedrooms, six bathrooms, two servants' quarters, three large social event spaces, along with all the other stuff that goes into a house?"

Samantha squeezed his arm. "It's never bothered you before."

Chase shrugged, then turned to Allison. "I hope you've been able to find your way around the house."

She smiled. "If not, Thor and Maya have helped me immensely."

They strolled into the mansion, and waiting for them was one of the servants. "Master Chase, we're glad to see you."

"Hi Roberto. How is the family?"

The short man with a graying beard smiled. "Wonderful."

"That's good to hear."

Roberto turned to Chase. "I will take your bags up to your room."

As he started to grab them, Chase touched his arm. "I can take care of it, but thanks. I'll sleep in the guest room."

Roberto smiled, then turned to Samantha. "Miss Samantha, the family is in the small dining room."

"Thank you, Roberto."

Chase set his bags in a corner. Samantha and the kids had already left for the dining room. Allison touched Chase's arm. "I can take the guest room."

He shook his head. "You already told me how much you enjoy the bed."

She grinned. "I really do. Why did you kiss me?"

He sighed. "I don't know if it was appropriate, but I did miss you."

She blushed and locked her arm in his. "It was appropriate."

They joined Samantha and the kids as they walked toward the living room. Chase chuckled to himself knowing that the room was larger than most people's houses.

"Chase, you're here."

"Mom, it's good to see you," Chase said as he hugged

her.

"And you too, son. I'm glad you changed your mind to join us."

Tricia turned to Allison. "Allison has been a joy to have with us."

"I'm glad to hear that." Chase greeted his four brothers, then grinned at Keenan. "I see you've moved from the chair."

Keenan laughed. "Yeah, I figured you were worth the move. How have you been?"

"Doing well. And you?"

"I actually found a woman who likes me. You'll see her tonight."

"Good for you."

"You have found yourself a beauty, Chase. Are you sure she's safe around the Connors?"

Chase shook his head. "We're just friends."

Micah joined them and spewed out a laugh. "Yeah, we can see that you two are friends."

They all turned when his father put his hand on his shoulder. "Son, it's good to see you. How's the bookstore business?"

"It's actually going pretty good, Dad. Thanks for asking."

Oliver Connor eyed his son for more than a moment. "You seem to be much better. Montana air must do that. Or is it this young beauty?" He tilted his head toward Allison.

Chase shook his head. "The Montana air is too darn cold right now. There have been two blizzards in the last two months."

Arthur, who resembled his father more than the other three boys, jumped in. "And you deliberately chose to move there."

Chase grinned and pointed at his temple. "Not too bright sometimes. I'm going to go unpack."

Allison joined him by the stairs.

He gazed at her. "Is everything okay?"

"Yeah, it's been going well here. I really like San Diego, and your family has been nice to me, but I've really missed you."

He stopped and faced her. "What does that mean?"

She shook her head. "I'm not sure, but I'm starting to figure it out."

After Allison helped Chase unpack, they joined the others in the pool area where the kids were swimming and the adults were lounging around. "One thing I've noticed is there is always a crowd here," Allison said.

Chase nodded. "The afternoons on the weekends are always packed with clients or business contacts who are trying to make a name with my family. For example, that man over there is Darius Carmen. He works with many top-notch performers, and he hopes to land a deal with Micah for attorney privileges for his clients. Good old Darius has been working at it for two years."

"You think he'd give it up after that long."

Chase grabbed a couple of glasses of wine as the host walked by. He handed one to Allison. "Carmen won't give up. Everyone knows my family is good at getting people off of major crimes or at least minimizing the sentence. Performers do have issues at times like everyone else." He sipped on his wine.

Allison pointed at a lovely lady talking with Keenan. "Another woman is trying to pick up your brother?"

Chase turned to where she was looking. "Yep, it's not uncommon to see that happen at these parties, and many times my brothers disappear for a couple of hours."

Allison frowned. "That's disgusting, but I've seen it at the Shepherd parties also. If I remember right, I tried to pick you up once. Guess I'm just as disgusting as the other gals."

Chase laughed. "See? You've already had a glimpse of what this life is like."

They both turned when a young woman with long

brown hair, brown eyes, and a shapely figure walked over to Chase. "Chase, I heard you were back in California. Why would you think of leaving California for Montana when you could have this anytime you wanted?" She stepped back and waved her hand over her body. Chase covered his mouth to keep from laughing.

Allison quickly locked arms with him. "Can't you see he's with me?"

The lady smirked. "The night's young." She strutted away.

Allison frowned at his chuckle. "You think that's funny?"

"No, but you wanted to know what my life was like, and this is it." Allison peered up at Chase. "Your family eats this up."

Chase sipped his drink. "One of the reasons I left California for Montana. Have you noticed how many guys have been eying you here?"

She drained the rest of her wine. "I'm not interested."

"Let's go for a walk."

"That would be lovely." Chase took her hand, led her out the back gate of the pool, and down a trail leading to the Pacific Ocean. Once on the sand, Allison slipped off her pumps and carried them. "It feels so good to feel the sand in my toes. I've walked along the beach each night since I've been here."

Once they reached the water, Chase bent down and took off his shoes.

"The water feels good," Allison said. "This is the first time I've ever walked in the Pacific Ocean, or any ocean for that matter, with a guy. Thank you for this."

They continued their trek, the waves undulating over their feet, for another fifteen minutes. Chase stopped and pointed to an area in the ocean. "See that area of rocks over there."

She nodded. "What is it?"

He took a deep breath. "That's suicide rock. Many believe that people jump to their death from there."

Allison's eyes widened. "What?"

"Yeah, it's a legend but there have been a few people who have killed themselves jumping off that rock for one reason or another."

A huge wave caused them to lose their balance, and they fell down into the sand. Allison laughed. Chase pulled her down into the sand and kissed her tenderly.

She opened her eyes and sat up. "You are going to make love with me right here on the beach?"

"Would that be a problem?"

She wrapped her arms around her knees. "It can't happen."

Chase looked at her. She stood up and frowned down at him. "It just can't happen."

Chapter 20

The next morning the others were gathered around the dining room table for breakfast when Allison entered the room. Keenan was the first one to greet her. "Allison, a sundress just won't work for our softball game today."

Allison eyed Chase who grinned. "I may have forgotten to tell you that the Connors are notorious for softball games."

"I'll change into something more appropriate."

Samantha walked by with some bagels. "Sorry, Allison, what you come downstairs with is what you wear for the morning softball game. You do look sharp, though, in a sundress and sandals, but of course you should be okay since you'll be on Chase's team. He wins all the time."

"That's because he cheats," Micah said. "Good morning, little brother, Allison. It should be interesting to see you play softball today."

Allison leaned over and whispered to Chase. "I've never played softball in my life. The only sports I've played were basketball and volleyball."

He whispered back. "Don't worry. The birthday girl gets final say on what we play, and she happens to like volleyball."

Once they'd filled their plates, Gracie sat next to Chase with Allison sitting on the other side of him. Oliver sat at the head of the table and Tricia at the other end. Chase turned to Gracie. "What game are we playing today, birthday girl?"

She grinned. "Volleyball of course."

"Volleyball it is—" her father said.

Samantha interrupted. "After you open your presents."

As if on cue, a couple of the servants brought the presents over.

Keenan grinned. "How many presents do you need?"

"Twenty-three to be exact," one of the servants said.

Gracie grinned. "I should get started."

Over the next thirty minutes, she opened the presents, with only one left to go. She grinned up at Chase. "You and Allison gave me a present?"

"We did," Chase said.

She tore open the wrapping, and her eyes widened at the box.

"It's a snow globe of the Rocky Mountains," Allison said. "Now when you miss your uncle, you can shake it up and see the snow over the mountains, and know that your uncle is shivering nearby."

"Thank you, Uncle Chase, Aunt Allison. I'm ready for sand volleyball."

The younger kids played on one volleyball court while the adults were on the sand volleyball court. Allison stood next to Chase, her sundress blowing in the wind. "This is crazy. Your family is beyond rich. You have sand all the way down to the ocean and beyond."

Oliver walked by and must have heard her comment. "This could be all yours, Allison."

Samantha came over. "Allison, you and Micah have been chosen as captains, and since you're new to the family, you get first choice."

Allison took a deep breath. "Of course, I choose Chase." Samantha, Dolly, and Keenan joined Allison's team.

"I'm way too old for this," Keenan said.

Samantha threw the volleyball at him. "Shut up and

serve." It drew a laugh from the rest. The two teams battled to a 1-1 tie. The third game would go to fifteen to see who the Connor champs were for the day. Allison served. The teams volleyed back and forth before she dove into the sand to bump it up to Chase, who slammed the ball over the net for the winning point.

Allison lifted her eyes up to Chase who had bent down to help her up. "Did we win?"

He smiled, snapping a photo with his cell phone. "You also won the photo-of-the-game contest."

"What?" she said, as he helped pull her up. He showed her the photo he'd taken. She laughed at the sand in her hair, face, and in her mouth. "I'll need a shower."

Chase lifted her up. "No dear, in California we do this." He carried her down to the ocean and dumped her into the water.

"Chase Connor, you jerk. Ouch, what was that?" Allison reached up and pulled him into the water, drawing a laugh from the remainder of the family. "How does it feel?"

He lifted her up and kissed her passionately. "Now that was wonderful."

That afternoon and into the evening, the Connors sat under umbrellas at the edge of the ocean enjoying themselves while Gracie, along with her nieces and nephews and her friends, had a birthday party at the pool near the house chaperoned by the servants.

"How is the antique store and bookstore going?" Samantha's husband, Steven, asked.

Chase sipped on his wine. "It's doing really well. I've made a profit every month in both stores; how that's happening I have no clue other than I think people are infatuated with something new."

"That's partially true," Arthur said. "I work with a lot of businesses, and they find that after the first six months or so, the initial attraction starts to slow down, then they have to find a new rebranding approach."

Samantha jumped in. "Chase, are you bringing your book collection back to Montana with you?"

He shook his head. "I'll leave it here for the nieces and nephews to read when they want."

Steven had another question. "I understand you helped the sheriff solve a mystery by clues left in a book. How did that work?"

"Yeah, I found some old books with some leads, clues—whatever you want to call them—to help give the sheriff more information. Many of the old books are about the history of Montana, the culture, that sort of thing. Smith Lake is one of the sources. It has so much history and so many mysteries that haven't been solved."
He held his glass with both hands. "The sheriff gave me a book that had eight mysteries in it that have never been solved in the county. We've solved two around Smith Lake with the help of many people, which is much appreciated."

Roderick peered over at Allison. "How did you two meet?"

She grinned. "Actually, it was at a diner where he was hitting on my former boyfriend's sister."

"I wasn't hitting on her," Chase said.

"Oh yes, you were, and we both know it. Even so, I didn't think much of Chase because I already had a boyfriend whom I thought would ask me to marry him someday. That never materialized, but I'm okay with it. Now, I'll figure out where to go for the rest of my life."

Oliver interrupted. "You can stay right here and work for the Connor Law Firm."

Allison shook her head. "Sorry, Mr. Connor, I saw what that was like with a friend of mine who was a paralegal. She spent countless hours supposedly working on cases, but mostly spent time with one of the attorneys." She tasted her wine once more. "I've learned a lot from Chase working for him the last couple of weeks at the bookstore. Mr. Connor, thanks for the job offer, but I already have a job as Chase's bookstore manager."

Chase eyed her. "You're coming back to Montana?"

She smiled. "Remember, I told you a couple of times to come here and get me. That meant I would be returning to Montana."

Tricia smiled. "There's something going on between the two of you."

Chase jumped in quickly. "We're business partners."

Samantha interrupted. "Chase, quit with the lies. We want to know what Allison thinks about you."

"Yes, ma'am," Chase grinned.

Allison took a deep breath. "There are so many things about Chase that I like. For instance, he's kind. An older lady called him up one day and asked if he would pick them up and bring them to the antique store, because they couldn't drive. He did it, and it started a craze around the town where he brings the senior citizens to the stores so they browse around. Most of the time they buy stuff."

Olivia nodded. "That sounds like Chase, but did you know he had all of this money?"

Samantha laughed. "Yeah, right, if you're talking about money. It's our grandfather who took care of that. But we all know that Chase is the bright bulb in the family."

Oliver laughed. "Then why is he running a bookstore?"

Chase sighed. "It's peaceful and quiet, and I don't have to worry about all the excess BS you have to put up with."

"That's true," Micah said. "But then we don't have to freeze our asses off."

Chase stood and pulled Allison up. "You have the best of all worlds. Allison, you feel like going for a walk?"

"You bet." She turned to the others. "Thanks for a wonderful evening."

Chase wrapped his arm around Allison. She grabbed his hand and peered into his eyes. "I enjoyed the time we had with your family. They are quirky, but they seem to care about you."

"You've only seen them when things are good. When things go the other way, you see a ruthless group of humans."

They walked in silence, enjoying the gentle breeze.

"About last night," Allison broke the silence.

"No need to say anything, I shouldn't have been that forward with you."

"It's not that at all. I've wanted you to be that way with me, but something's happened that I have to tell you about. Can we sit somewhere and talk?"

He eyed her. "In the sand?"

She smiled. "I'm okay with getting sand up my you know what. It's important that we have this conversation."

"Sounds serious."

"It is, and I'm scared to talk to you about it."

They sat in the sand and Allison pulled his arm around her shoulders. "I didn't tell you everything that happened that night with Willis." Tears started streaming down her eyes. "He raped me that night, and I'm afraid to make love with you because of what happened. I'm afraid it will bring back all that happened that night, and I'll hate you for trying to do it to me."

Chase wiped away her tears. "Did you talk to Olivia?"

"I did. She set me up with the family doctor who checked to see if I was pregnant. I'm thankful I'm not. Also, she checked around down there and told me it's possible I couldn't have children."

Chase encircled with both his arms and brought her head to his chest. "I'm so sorry. You really need to think about filing charges against him."

"It's over with. I don't want to go through the horror again. I came here to get my life back together and I am. I'm moving past that night, but I'm just worried about you."

"What do you mean?"

She sighed. "I want you in my life, but why would you want a woman who can't provide a family? But I don't even know if you're thinking like that."

He gently wiped away her tears. "No question I missed you while you were gone. I'd hoped that you would find some peace and happiness in your life while you were here. It sounds like you have."

She nodded. "I didn't want to come here, but I'm glad I did. I found out so much about myself that I didn't know. For so long I've been lonely, so I attached myself to Willis, even though I knew we didn't belong together." She moved closer to him. "I was truthful when I told you I loved you— not because I'm lonely but because you make me feel special. We can talk about anything, and my heart beats faster when you're around me. I hope you feel the same."

Chase kissed her on the forehead. "I promised I'd come and bring you back to Montana. The reason why is I want to be with you. I've never thought about children; it wouldn't be a good thing for me because I'm a Connor." He shifted her to lock eyes with him. "You don't know what will happen. I heard you say the doctor *thought* you may not be able to have children, but that's not a guarantee. We'll cross that path when we come to it, but I do want you to come back and work with me at the bookstore."

Her dreamy eyes stared into his. "Is that all?"

Chapter 21

The next morning Chase and Allison were the first ones downstairs for breakfast. Minutes later Chase's parents walked in and joined them.

"Your flight is in a couple of hours?" Oliver asked.

Chase didn't say anything because he had food in his mouth. "No, we're not going back until tomorrow. We plan on taking my nieces and nephews on a cruise of the San Diego Harbor."

"They'll enjoy that," Tricia said. "That's considerate of you. Have you thought any more about where you two are heading?"

Allison smiled. "I'm going back to manage the bookstore. We'll see where it takes us from there."

Oliver finished a sip of his coffee. "I can see you two care a lot about each other."

They turned when Roderick waltzed in. "Isn't this awfully early for you, Chase?" Roderick asked.

"Nope, I'm used to it because I have businesses to run, much different than going to the attorney office at ten."

Roderick grinned. "There is that."

Gracie came bounding over to Chase and Allison. "I'm sorry to see you guys leave today. I'll miss you, Uncle Chase."

Chase hugged his niece. "We're going to stick around another day because we have a surprise for all of the nieces and nephews, so eat some breakfast because we have things to do."

Later that morning, the nieces and nephews joined Chase and Allison for a ride around San Diego Bay. Once they embarked on the boat, Allison purchased snacks for each of the children. Fortunately, the seven kids stayed close to the two adults. The youngest boy, Race, who was Samantha's son, held Allison's hand throughout the ride.

She bent down to talk to him. "Are you okay?"

"I'm afraid of the water."

She rubbed his short, blond hair. "I'm right here with you."

The cruise started around the bay. They passed by the *Star of India*. "That's an old boat," Micah's oldest daughter said.

"It is," Chase said. "Did you hear the guide say it's the world's oldest active sailing ship?"

She peered up at him. "He said it started sailing in 1863."

"That's right. It started its life with two difficult voyages to India." The others had gathered around Chase to hear the story he was telling. "On the first trip there was a collision and also a mutiny."

"What's a mutiny?" one of the children asked.

"The crew decided to rebel against their leaders."

"That's sad," Race said. They all nodded.

Chase continued. "On its second voyage, a cyclone hit the ship near India and tore up those large topmasts there." He pointed. "They did make it to port, but it was tough."

The group turned to the guide's voice once more. "We are passing the Coronado Bridge, which links San Diego and Coronado."

"What does link mean?" Race asked.

Allison knelt down, pointing at the bridge. "See how the bridge goes across the water from one area to another. Link means the bridge connects two cities, in this case San Diego and Coronado."

"Look at all the ships over there," an older boy said, pointing toward the ships.

"It's pretty cool," Chase said. "Listen."

The tour guide spoke. "There are more than sixty U.S. Naval ships in the port."

"Wow, that is a lot of ships. Do they protect the United States?" the older boy said.

"They sure do."

They passed Shelter Island Shoreline Park. The kids were starting to wind down because of the fresh air and all the excitement of the ride. Gracie took Chase's hand. "The adults are missing all the fun."

"They sure are," he smiled.

Gracie pointed to a monument high on a hill. "What is that?"

"Cabrillo National Monument," Chase said. "It is located on the southern tip of the peninsula and celebrates the first explorer way back in September 1542. Juan Rodriquez Cabrillo was the first European explorer to visit the West Coast of the United States."

"He must be very old," one of the younger kids said.

Chase grinned. "He is that."

Chase and Allison brought the kids back to the mansion around eight. They ran out of the limo and hurried into the facility to find their parents who were in the pool area. When Chase and Allison joined them, they were all telling stories about what had happened during the afternoon.

Allison linked Chase's arm. "That was fun, and it was good to spend time with your nieces and nephews."

Chase kissed her on the cheek. "It was," he said. "Did you enjoy yourself?"

"I did because I was with you." She took a deep breath and spoke softly. "Someday, I want to try to have a child with you. When I'm ready."

Tricia turned to them. "Just in time. We're taking a

family photo since this is the first time we've had everyone with their better halves together." She directed where she wanted everyone. After that was done, others shot several photos of the family members with their children.

After the kids were in bed, Olivia turned to Chase and Allison who were sitting on the edge of the pool kicking their feet in the water. "The kids couldn't stop talking about how much fun they had on the cruise. Thank you."

"No problem," Chase said. "It was a lot of fun."

Samantha grinned. "Little brother. you may have to watch out because your nephew is cozying up to Allison. He told Steven and me that her hand was so soft."

Allison smiled. "He is a handsome little guy, but then all of the Connor men and boys are a handsome lot."

They all laughed. "Way to wiggle your way into the Connor family," Roderick said. "I'm sure Dad was glad to hear that since he's getting on in years."

Tricia chuckled. "Aren't we all."

It drew a laugh from the group. Keenan, who was sitting next to his girlfriend, threw a beach ball at Chase. "What is it with you and these books? I've read that you're helping the sheriff solve some crimes in Montana."

Chase threw it back at him. "They're different kinds of mysteries. Granted some have turned into crimes, like kidnapping and trafficking, to name a couple, but the books deal with some really old ones."

Olivia leaned forward on her chaise lounge. "Explain how you are figuring these things out from a book?"

Chase sipped on his glass of wine, which was sitting near him. "As my family knows, I do a lot of reading, and when I read these books, I pull out words or sentences or paragraphs that may be clues to some old happenings in the area—usually out in the brush. For instance, there was a passage about the sighting of what some have called Bigfoot along Smith Lake, which is a lake near the town of Mountain Ridge. The passage talked about water near a frozen lake, and we went to the area it was talking about, and there we found unfrozen water and bones."

"What?" Oliver asked, his eyes wide.

"Yeah, the rest of the lake was frozen, but that little bit, maybe about a body width, wasn't iced over. Why it was unfrozen is something they're looking into. In another passage in the same book, it connects 'Nessie' with 'Flessie.' As many of you know, 'Nessie' is said to be located in Scotland, but someone saw something in the water in Flathead Lake, and they called it Flessie."

He took another sip. "With those two passages I was able to connect Smith Lake and Flathead Lake together, meaning there was a possible underground connection between the two lakes that people may have used for transporting drugs and other items without being seen."

"Amazing," Micah said. "Has anything come out of it?"

"Not at this point, but then the sheriff's department is busy dealing with other issues around the county. Flathead County is the fourth most populous county in the state and is one of the larger ones in land area, so there is a lot of space to cover. Plus, it is close to Canada which adds another difficult layer."

Samantha tasted her beer. "It sounds like you've found your niche, Chase. Good for you. Will you ever come back to California?"

Chase took a deep breath. "I'll never say never, but right now I'm happy running the bookstore and antique store." He stood up and grabbed Allison's hand. "Do you feel like going for a walk along the beach?"

"Always."

They had walked for about ten minutes, when Chase pulled her down into the sand and wrapped his arm around her. She snuggled into him. "See the whale over there?"

She quickly searched where he was pointing. "I see it. That's amazing."

"This spot is where you can see whales every once in a

while. There's a lot we can take from a whale."

"What?" she lifted her eyes to him.

"For instance, a whale can encourage us to listen to our inner voices, as well as follow our unique paths with courage and faith. Right now, we're worried about what direction we're going in our lives because of what has happened. Many believe a whale has spiritual symbolism which signifies inner truth, spiritual guidance, and an ability to navigate through our emotions."

Allison planted a kiss on his cheek. "You continue to amaze me." She pushed him down on the sand and kissed him. Just as she started to lift up her dress she stopped and sat up. "I'm sorry. I shouldn't have done that."

He peered into her eyes. "It's okay. Someday, you'll be ready."

Her eyes widened. "You mean you would make love with me after what happened?"

"Of course, I would, but only when you're ready. I do care a lot about you—not just sexually, but I care about your mind, your attitude, your smile, and so many other things."

She kissed him. "That makes it so much easier for me, knowing that you think of me more than just a woman you can sleep with." She peered into his eyes. "I love you."

Chapter 22

On Wednesday morning, it was close to nine, when Allison hurried down the stairs to see how Chase was doing in the bookstore. She had enjoyed her week in California and told Chase she wanted to go back again, but this time with him.

Allison was feeling so much better about herself, and even told herself that one of these nights she would climb into bed with Chase and would never leave. She just hoped he would feel the same way.

"Ms. Allison, you decided to wake up."

"Good morning, Milo, how have you been?"

He hugged her. "Wonderful, but we missed you."

"We?"

He smiled. "Yes, many customers came through asking for you. I told them you're on a much-needed vacation but would be back soon."

"I did enjoy myself but am glad to be back with you and the others."

"Did you get married?"

Her eyes widened. "Why would you say something like that?"

He grinned. "I see the way you and Chase eye each other."

She smiled. "Sorry, Milo, we're nowhere near anything

like that. We're just business partners. If we do go any further, you'll be the first one to know. Right now, I have to get to work." Allison walked into the bookstore and stopped when she saw Chase on a ladder. "There you are. You're always on that ladder stocking books on the shelves."

He smiled down at her. "Morning. You decided to join me."

"I slept wonderfully last night; however, the bed isn't half as nice as the California bed I slept in."

He stepped down. "Funny you should say that, but the bed is on its way to Montana as we speak."

She gazed at him. "What did you do?"

"Well, you said you liked the bed, and it was just sitting there, so I had Samantha ship it to you, so you have your wonderful bed to sleep in."

She reached over and kissed him. "Thank you so much. I'll enjoy it." She stopped. "Hold it, it's your bed."

"It is, but you can have it for the time being."

She lifted her eyes at him. "What are you saying?"

He took a deep breath. "Well, if you decide maybe you'd like me around more, then we'll share the bed."

She batted her eyes. "Count on it." Her smile vanished.

"What's wrong?" Chase asked.

"I have to do it. I have to talk to Willis and tell him I'm over him, that he can't control me anymore."

"Are you sure you're ready?"

She nodded. "I have to if I want to move forward, and I do want to move on with my life."

During the morning, when she took a break, Allison called Willis, who agreed to meet her at the bar and grill for lunch. It was close to noon when she told Chase she was heading to lunch.

He took her hand. "Are you going to be okay?"

She smiled. "I hope so, but I have to do this. Olivia told me this is an important step."

It was ten minutes after twelve when Allison arrived at

the bar and grill. She found Willis sitting sipping on his water when she walked in. When she joined him, he jumped out of his seat to hug her.

"I'm glad you called me," he said when she backed up. "I had no clue where you disappeared to, and I was afraid something had happened to you."

She sat down. "I needed to get away for a while, and I had a wonderful time."

"Where did you go?"

"A place where I feel comfortable and will go back again."

Jake brought a menu over. "Good to see you again, Allison. Where have you been?"

She smiled. "Let's just say I enjoyed myself immensely."

Jake grinned. "I'm glad to hear that. The special today is a fish sandwich with fries."

"That will work for me," Allison said, "with a lemonade."

Jake turned to Willis. "Would you like to look at the menu?"

"No, I'll just have a burger and fries with a beer."

Once he left, Willis reached for Allison's hands, but she pulled back. "You're not glad to see me?"

Allison took a deep breath. "I called you to tell you in person that we're through. I had time to think about where my life is going, and I know it won't include you." She leaned toward him so she could lower her voice. "What you did to me was despicable. You raped me, and the only reason I don't turn you into the cops is because I want to move on, and I'm over you and your family."

Willis's eyes were smoking. "What have I told you about breaking away from a Shepherd?"

"You don't scare me anymore, Willis. You're a brute, a womanizer, and a woman abuser, among other things. I feel sorry for your pathetic life with your family, and I don't want to be part of it. In fact, I never did love you; I was just afraid of you and your father, but I'm not anymore. There is nothing you or your family can do to me. You've already done enough damage." She'd said enough.

Willis stood up. "We'll see about that." He stormed out of the bar and grill. Jake brought their meals over. "What did you say?"

Allison smiled. "I finally got enough guts to tell the son of a bitch I didn't need him in my life."

"Good for you. I'll take the lunch away."

She shook her head. "Can you box both of them up? I'll take the other lunch to Chase. He's always hungry."

~

Chase noticed Sheriff Portal was fidgety as he drank his glass of wine. "What are you doing here at the bar?" Chase asked, walking over to him.

He frowned. "Damned if I know. My wife believes I should attend some of these important events, but we both know it's all about the Shepherds finding someone else to suck up to."

Allison joined the two. She had heard the last part. "Now, Sheriff, that isn't nice of you to say about our hosts."

The sheriff huffed. "Allison, you know that's exactly who the Shepherd family is." He looked at her. "Why are you wearing that low cut dress? You're showing everything."

Allison laughed. "Now, Sheriff, I'll never tell." She laughed once more when the sheriff turned beet red. Allison handed Chase a drink. The sheriff rolled his eyes. "Are you his servant because you work at the bookstore?"

"Why would you ask something like that?"

"It's just I can't remember you doing anything like that for Willis."

She frowned. "I didn't like Willis as much as I do my boss."

Chase changed the subject. "Is there a special reason for

any of this tonight?"

Allison took his hand. "The sheriff is right; the Shepherds hold these events to find people with money. For instance, Mr. Grenham has been at many of these events, and Mr. Shepherd has tried to rope him into different projects."

The sheriff joined in. "I've heard of Mr. Grenham. Isn't he the guy who owns all those food distribution companies in the area?"

Allison nodded. "He is worth a lot of money. Mr. Shepherd wants to use his distribution system for this new resort that may or may not go through. Right now, Mr. Grenham isn't for it."

"Why?" Chase asked.

Allison squeezed Chase's hand. "*Your* family is said to be involved in it. Mr. Grenham also works with the Native American reservations around the region and has seen firsthand how your family has mishandled the people on the reservations. As a result, he'll never be part of the organization."

"I'd like to meet this guy."

Allison glanced at him. "Are you sure? He may not say a word to you once he finds out who you are."

He kissed her on the forehead. "Ye of little faith."

"Okay, I'll introduce you to him."

"Talk to you later, Sheriff," Chase said.

"I'll be right here."

~

Hand in hand, Allison and Chase walked over to Mr. Grenham. The tall gentleman in a cowboy hat, who had been talking to a couple of other business owners, noticed them. "Excuse me," he told the men. "Allison Winters, you look more radiant than I've ever seen you. How have you been? Why aren't you hanging out with Willis? Did you finally get smart and dump the snobbish prick?"

Allison laughed. "Right there. How have you been?"

"Wonderful. I know that Mr. Shepherd wants money

from me, but he'll never get it. However, I do enjoy the social event because I get to make more contacts." Mr. Grenham eyed Chase. "I've seen you somewhere, but I can't place it."

Allison took a deep breath. "This is Chase Connor, who runs the bookstore and antique store in Mountain Ridge."

The man glared at Chase. "The only reason I'm even saying anything to you is because you are with Allison."

Chase grinned. "It must have a lot to do with my family, in particular my father, Oliver. It seems he rubs a lot of people the wrong way all the time."

"You could say that. I want nothing to do with him or his family." He started to turn away, but Chase's voice stopped him. "I understand you're a good businessman and won't walk away without at least hearing what one has to offer even if it is a Connor."

The man stopped and turned to Chase. "You have two minutes."

"I'll make it simple for you, Mr. Grenham, and it probably won't make either of us a lot of money, but my bookstore continues to grow. However, it doesn't have enough Native American materials to help those in the area learn about their culture. You have a distribution network which could possibly help me bring in these types of books from Native American reservations. In addition, I want to start a reading program for Native Americans on the reservations and in the bookstore. Done in less than two minutes."

"A minute to be exact," Mr. Grenham said. "I'll be in Mountain Ridge for the next two days." He handed him a card. "Call me and we'll discuss possibilities."

Once he left, Allison hugged Chase. "I'm proud of you. That's a wonderful idea."

They turned to Nathan Shepherd's voice. "Allison, you didn't take long in finding another lover after dumping my son."

Allison smiled. "It's nothing like that. I hugged Chase because I'm proud of the fact that he was able to provide Mr. Grenham with a proposal that the guy actually liked. I believe you've been trying for at least a couple of years, but nothing has panned out."

Shepherd glared at Chase. "If he's smart, he'll stay away from the Connors."

Chase's lips formed into a smirk. "Aren't you trying to work something out with my family on this resort project? How is that going?"

"We're near making a deal. It's just a matter of time before everything gets underway and there's a major announcement." Nathan Shepherd whipped around and disappeared into the crowd.

Allison chuckled. "He's a liar. There is nothing happening with the resort."

"How do you know that?"

Allison finished her wine before speaking. "He would be bragging about it to anyone and everyone. At this point, the resort probably is dead, but he'll continue to find a way to make it work."

"There you are, Chase."

"Sheriff, is everything okay?" Chase turned toward him.

He sighed. "Another sighting of our Bigfoot today, and we're going out tomorrow to see if we can find anything. I hope you will join us."

"What time?"

The sheriff smiled. "I'll make sure it's after ten."

"Why so late?" Chase asked.

"Because you definitely need your beauty sleep."

Allison grinned. "I'll attest to that. He's up by seven."

The sheriff's head tilted toward her. "How would you know?"

Allison blushed. "I sleep in the extra room in his apartment, so I hear him moving around in the morning."

"Yeah, right."

"Think what you want, but I'll have rolls and coffee ready for you when you show up."

Chapter 23

The sheriff and a couple of deputies arrived several minutes before nine at the bookstore. "Where are the rolls?" one of the deputies asked, as they walked in.

"Right here," Allison said, setting them down on the table in the bookstore. The law enforcement officials sat down at the table and dug in.

"These rolls are very good," the sheriff said.

"Thank you," Allison said.

One of the deputies said, "You are so fortunate to be with Chase."

Another jumped in. "Allison, what happened to you and Willis?"

"That's over with."

"And now you're with Chase?" another asked.

Allison shook her head. "I'm his bookstore manager, and I'm just helping him out this morning because I know the sheriff seems to have a large appetite. It makes me wonder if his wife can cook!"

Everyone laughed and the sheriff growled. "You know darn well my wife can cook well since you've eaten many times at our house."

Allison grinned. "That's true, and she is a good cook, but you really do need to relax, Sheriff, or you'll have a heart attack right in front of us." Just then Chase joined them, his hair wet from a shower.

They spent the next half hour chatting. The sheriff stood up. "We're burning daylight."

The group headed out the door. "Bring my boss home safely?" Allison said, winking at Chase.

The sheriff laughed. "He'll probably be the one bringing us home safely."

~

The sheriff had broken up the search into two areas. The deputies would handle the path above the cabins while he and Chase would search the tree line once more. As they were driving, the sheriff spoke to Chase, "What is it with you two?"

"It's no one's business what goes on between Allison and me."

The sheriff eyed him. "I can understand what happened with her and Willis, but what's holding you back?"

Chase sighed. "I'm a Connor, and the family has had all kinds of issues over the years from infidelity to working with corrupt politicians to helping criminals get off with lighter sentences than they deserve."

The sheriff headed up the mountain toward Smith Lake. "I've run across people like that all my life, and, Chase, you are not one of those people. Everyone who sees you two together knows you two love each other. Would you ever consider cheating on Allison?"

"No, but there's still the Connor name."

"The reason you're in Montana is because you were tired of helping criminals get off. You could have represented Dr. Boyd, but you chose not to. When I met my wife, I knew I wanted to be with her for the rest of my life." He chuckled. "We'd only known each other a week when I asked her to marry me, and we've been together for thirty years. You're a bright guy, and you realize we're not promised tomorrow, so marry her."

The sheriff stopped because they couldn't go any further. Climbing out of the cruiser, they walked up the path toward the tree line. They arrived up there ten minutes later and stopped so the sheriff could take a breather. Chase searched the area while the sheriff sat on a rock and took a swig of his canteen.

"Do you see anything?"

"I'm just thinking about the rocks where the footprints stopped. There is something that we're not seeing there, and we need to take a closer look when we reach that place."

"I agree." He stood up. "I'm ready."

They arrived at the rocks fifteen minutes later and started searching the area for anything that would help them. Chase hiked up a hill of rocks. As he got higher, he noticed a bunch of broken ones. He knelt down and started removing the rocks.

Several minutes later, he saw a hole. As he removed more rocks, the hole became larger. He hollered down to the sheriff. "I've found what looks like a hole in the rocks." As the sheriff crawled up closer, Chase helped him.

"I'm getting too old to climb around in these rocks," the sheriff said. "What do we have?" Chase knelt next to it and pointed at it. "It's possible someone could have jumped down into it, but how would the rocks have covered the hole once more?"

"Unless there are more than one involved."

Sheriff Portal rolled his eyes. "More than one Bigfoot?"

Chase shook his head. "I'm not saying that. What if there is a creature of sorts, and a human is protecting it?"

The sheriff scratched his head. "The only thing I know is we'll get someone else to search this cavern." He sat down and hit his phone calling for a search team to join them. "Now we just sit back and wait."

While waiting, Chase started removing more rocks opening the hole, and within the next fifteen minutes he was able to see more clearly down into the hole. "It sure looks like there are bones down there."

The sheriff crawled over to look down. He grabbed his

flashlight and shined it down into the hole. "It sure does look like those are bones."

They turned when the deputies joined them. "What did you find?" one asked. The sheriff took control. "We're not exactly sure other than we may have found some bones."

The deputy's search team joined them. The sheriff explained to them what they found. The team set up some rope to lower a member down into the cave along with the sheriff. The sheriff eyed the team leader. "I'd like Chase to join us."

"Sure thing, Sheriff."

The three donned helmets with lights before they were lowered into the cavern. Their first task was to gather up the bones and mark them.

While they did that, Chase followed a tunnel that led to a different location. He traveled a couple of hundred feet when he came upon a fork and chose the one on the left. Another five hundred feet and he started to see light—an opening. Hurrying to it, he stepped outside the cave and looked around.

Where was he?

Chase walked down a trail but kept within sight of the cave entrance. He stopped when he saw smoke from a cabin chimney.

A voice behind had him whipping around.

"You shouldn't be here."

"Why?"

A short man with long hair and a long beard stood in front of him. "This is the creature's habitat, and he doesn't like visitors."

"Then why are you here?"

Before the man could say anything, Chase heard a screech, like the one in the Bernard house and at the cabin a couple of days ago. He spun around and saw a humongous person or something else. Then he felt a prick in his neck. He slapped at it, and his eyes fought to stay open. "What did you do to me?"

"Joshua needs to feed."

Voices murmured in the distance. A shot rang out. He fell.

The first thing he saw when he opened his eyes was Allison whose face was mere inches from his. Her face seemed to ebb and flow like a wave.

"You're awake."

He blinked and looked around—white upon white upon white. "Where am I?"

She held his hands. "You're in the hospital."

"How—I don't remember what happened."

"Honey, you were drugged, but the sheriff saved your life."

"How? What?"

"I'll let the sheriff explain. He'll be here soon." She wiped tears off her cheeks. "What were you thinking? I could have lost you."

They turned to a cough. The sheriff stood in the door, holding his hat in his hands. "I'm sorry to disturb you two lovebirds."

Allison stood up. "I'm going to get coffee." She walked by and hugged the lawman. "Thank you for saving his life." She hurried out.

The sheriff pulled a chair near Chase. "She was really worried about you. I don't think she left your side."

"What day is it?"

"Wednesday afternoon. The long-haired man's name is Zachary Bowdle who has been living in those mountains for the past twenty years. He ran into Joshua Bernard when he was twelve after the Bernards threw him out of the house."

Chase's eyes widened, then he cringed and rubbed the back of his neck.

The sheriff nodded. "You were right. The Bernards have another son." Sheriff Portal continued. "Joshua didn't know any better because he and Gideon always played games, but then Joshua started killing animals for kicks. Then once he got nasty with his mother, and they threw him out. Seems he doesn't know boundaries."

Chase sipped water from his straw, his eyes remaining on the sheriff.

"Joshua and Bowdle met, and Bowdle took him in. At first, he raised Joshua to help scavenge for food, then something snapped in Bowdle, and that's when he devised the Bigfoot scheme. It turned deadly when Joshua started preying on humans. It was Bowdle who used a knockout drug on you."

"Wow."

The sheriff nodded. "DNA tests show at least bones from three different humans in the tunnel, but there are a lot more down there. We're not sure what type at this point. Any way you look at it, Bowdle is going away for a long time and Joshua may get the death penalty, if they don't prove he's insane."

"How did I survive?"

"The deputy and I came out the cave opening and saw Bowdle stick something in your neck. Bowdle told the creature to run away, but the deputy shot him in the leg knocking him down. Joshua let out a deafening screech which almost broke our eardrums. Finally, we were able to subdue him after we handcuffed Bowdle."

The sheriff swigged down some water. "We searched Bowdle's cabin, and you were right—there were snow shoes that made the feet appear larger than normal. To spare himself any long-term prison time or even possibly the death sentence, Bowdle confessed that at first it was just an elaborate scheme to scare people away from the area. He never did admit why, but my guess is it had something to do with the resort."

"That would mean others could be involved?" Chase said.

"Possibly, but right now this is over."

"What about the book?"

Sheriff Portal rubbed his beard. "What do you mean?"

"The book is at least fifteen years old, meaning that if its contents are true, the guy has been hunting for at least fifteen years, or is the book version something altogether different?"

"That's a good question. I don't know if we can answer it, but my best guess is we have the culprit because it's the same area where people have claimed to have seen Bigfoot."

"You could be right, which means we solved two mysteries out of that book. Two down and half a dozen to go."

The sheriff laughed. "Take it easy. Go take care of that young woman of yours. I've said this a couple of times—marry her and start a family."

They both turned when Allison walked in. She stopped and stared at them. "Is Chase okay?"

The sheriff smiled. "Your stubborn-as-a-mule man will be just fine. I should be going."

After he left, Allison sat near Chase. "Are you feeling better? The nurse said there is a possibility you could leave tomorrow."

"I'm ready. Don't know how I'll be able to tell Mr. Grenham what happened since I missed that meeting."

"No worries, dear love, I contacted him and explained what had happened. He stopped by the hospital yesterday afternoon, and we discussed your thoughts about the reading program and the books. Mr. Grenham plans on bringing the idea back to his board meeting on Monday. I'm guessing it'll be a go."

He grinned. "Where would I be without you?"

She squeezed his hand. "That's what a good bookstore manager does, among other things."

Chapter 24

Over the remainder of the week, Allison made sure Chase took it easy, working on getting his strength back. She handled the bookstore while also checking on him in the apartment every few hours. Although it wasn't easy.

"Are you really going to check on me every hour on the hour?" Chase groused on Friday.

"Someone's gotta make sure you're okay. I almost lost you, and that won't happen again. Also, I told the sheriff he needs to keep you out of any of his investigations."

Chase rolled his eyes.

"I mean it, Chase. My heart almost exploded when the EMTs rushed you into the hospital. They said your heart had stopped."

"I'm okay," he said, pulling her near him.

"I'm going to do everything in my power to make sure that happens. What do you want for lunch?"

He pulled her onto his lap and kissed her. She started to respond but backed off and waved her finger. "It's not going to work. Now what do you want to eat?"

An hour later, after the two finished their tuna sandwiches, Allison headed back downstairs. That night she and Chase sat on the couch eating popcorn.

"Allison, you can't hover over me forever. I realize it scared you. but I still have to live my life."

She peered into his eyes. "I don't want to lose you."

"You won't." He kissed her.

"I had better not." She kissed him back then laid her head on his chest and fell asleep.

~

Chase had just opened the bookstore on Saturday morning when Xavier and Anastasia walked in. "Good morning, Boss, we stopped by to grab a couple of books to help with one of our history projects that we have to do for school," Xavier said.

"Doesn't the school library have books like that?"

The young redhead with freckles, who was much shorter than Xavier's six-five height, said, "Mr. Connor, Xavier said he's seen some books here that are much better than the school has to offer."

"What specifically are you looking for?" Chase asked.

Xavier explained. "We need to do some research for a play we're writing on the happenings around Smith Lake."

"What exactly?" Chase asked.

"Supposedly there have been some sightings of either Bigfoot or some large animal around the lake over the years," Anastasia said.

"In the lake or outside the lake?" Chase asked.

"Mostly inside the lake," Xavier said.

Chase sighed. "You realize most of the lake is frozen right now because it's February."

"Not all. There is an area that doesn't stay completely frozen, and many believe it leads to an underground tunnel."

"You expect to find all that out of a book?"

"Why not?" the girl asked. "You solved the Bernard house case with a book, so we figured we'd try also."

"Xavier knows where the books are, so go ahead and take a look."

After thirty minutes of searching, they didn't seem to find anything, and Chase could tell they were close to giving up.

"You know sometimes the best research is going to the

source."

Their eyes widened. "Going to the lake?" Xavier said.

"I wouldn't advise it, but yeah, you may find something out onsite. Also, I do have a book that has unsolved mysteries I'll let you browse through, but it doesn't leave the bookstore."

"Understood," Xavier said. Chase went up to his apartment, grabbed the book out of the safe, and brought it back down to the kids.

"Thanks, Mr. Connor," Anastasia said. "We're going to do some reading."

Chase left the two at a corner table. He was working on an inventory when a text came through. *What do you want for lunch? Allison.*

He texted back. *Surprise me.*

After breakfast, Allison had waved goodbye, saying she was going to Kalispell to purchase some groceries, along with some clothes for herself.

Chase was beginning to realize Allison was going to be a significant part of her life. But was she ready? He turned when the two high school students came hurrying over from the table.

"Chase, I think we may have found something." Both teens' eyes lit up.

"Calm down and explain to me what you have found."

Xavier opened to a page in the book that talked about a sea serpent or something of that nature in Flathead Lake. "The rumor is that Flathead Lake and Smith Lake connect underground somehow, so why wouldn't it be possible for uncommon species to drift into Smith Lake?"

Chase thought for a moment. "Xavier, that's pretty iffy. We're talking about creatures that are supposedly extinct, but I've seen some strange things since I've been here, so if you don't mind, I'll check this out with you."

"You will, Mr. Connor?" Anastasia said.

He grinned. "As long as you call me Chase." He

grabbed another book off the shelf. "This one talks about myths and legends. If I remember right, I read about Flessie in this book."

The two high school students' faces were confused at the name.

"Did you two ever read about Nessie, Loch Ness monster in Scotland? They're calling the serpent here in Flathead Lake, Flessie, and according to this book, eighty-one or even more now unusual sightings have occurred on Flathead Lake. I have a couple of ideas. How about I contact a friend of mine who works at the University of Montana. He's an historian who focuses on the history of Montana. I bet he'd take a ride out to the area of Smith Lake that you were talking about."

They all turned when the bookstore door opened. Allison hurried in. "If I had known Xavier and Anastasia would be here, I would have brought more lunch."

Chase grinned. "We can pick up something on the way." He grabbed her hand. "You guys ready?"

"I have to put the groceries away first, dear."

"I'll help you," Chase said.

Fifteen minutes later they were finished and heading out the door. "What is going on?" Allison asked.

"I'll explain later."

They all hopped in the Jeep and drove toward Smith Lake. During the summer the lake was crowded with locals who enjoyed fishing, boating, and other outdoor activities.

"The site that we're talking about is along one of the three wetlands that surround the lake," Xavier said. "There is usually as much as four inches of frozen water, so we should be okay. We found a spot that is not frozen, so maybe that's where Flessie is."

Chase drove as far as the road allowed. "I guess we hoof it from here. Remember to stay on the trail." Chase led the way hiking into the wetland area. It was thirty minutes later when he suddenly stopped. "I think we've found what we're looking for."

Xavier almost bumped into him. "What is it?"

"I have no idea, but have a gander at those bones." Chase called the sheriff who answered promptly. "Sheriff, you need to see this."

~

The sheriff and one of his deputies arrived close to an hour later. They found Chase, Allison, and the two kids eating sandwiches. "So, you decided to have a late lunch on Smith Lake near a wetlands? What next, Chase?"

Allison finished eating her sandwich. "Chase and I are trying to find unique dating experiences to see if we're compatible together."

"Ugh," the sheriff said.

Chase grinned. "You asked me to update you on mysteries concerning the book. Well, this kind of deals with the book."

"*Kind of?*" the sheriff frowned.

Chase finished his sandwich and wiped his mouth. "In the book, the author talks about Flessie, which is a play on words stemming from the 'Nessie' in Scotland. Anyway, Xavier and Anastasia are doing a project involving the serpent, and I told them there have been more than eighty sightings on Flathead Lake."

"We're nowhere near Flathead Lake."

"Correct, but what if there was an underground system so that large fish could swim between the lakes?"

The sheriff stared at Chase with a scowl.

"You think I'm crazy, Sheriff, but where did those bones come from?"

The sheriff's eyes widened. "Bones?"

"Yes," Chase said, pointing to the path a few feet from where they ate their lunch.

The sheriff and his deputy slowly moved toward the bones. "They look like human bones," the deputy said.

Sheriff Portal hit his phone. "Dispatch, contact

emergency crews and get them out to these coordinates." After he ended the call, he turned to Chase and the others. "Okay, explain to me what is happening here?"

Chase shrugged. "There isn't much else to tell you. You wanted help solving mysteries out of that book, so here I am."

"Damn it, Chase. This is not from that book. This is something totally different."

"How do you know, Sheriff?"

The sheriff shook his head. "We'll take it from here. Besides, you need to go to the big resort discussion at the convention center in a couple of hours."

"It's not at the Shepherds' house?" Allison asked.

"Nope, the Connors didn't want the people to think it was all about the Shepherds, which is smart for the support they're hoping to gain for this project."

Chase sighed. "My father is always thinking about how to make a buck."

Chapter 25

Chase jumped when the doorbell buzzed. He reached for the box to see who it was and saw the sheriff's waving hand. Chase pushed the button to talk to him. "You're up awfully early," he said.

"I am, but I have some news for you. If you let me in, we can discuss it."

"I'll be right down," Chase said, as he buzzed the sheriff in. He walked out to the living room where Allison was sleeping on the couch. He sat down on the side and blew in her face, watching her bat the air with her hands. Her eyes finally popped open.

"What are you doing?"

"You looked so cute swiping at the air."

She sat up. "I must have fallen asleep watching a show on one of your three channels on your television."

Chase grinned. "You always make it a point to tell me how I need to buy a Roku."

She grinned and took off the blanket revealing her nightgown. "Have you gotten the message yet?"

"By the way, the sheriff is on his way up."

She jumped off the couch and wrapped herself in the blanket. "I'm half naked."

He grinned. "I've always said you're gorgeous in the morning." Chase watched as she hurried into her bedroom to get some clothes on. She came out of her bedroom brushing her hair into a ponytail. "Is the sheriff always like this?"

"He can be when he has something important to say. By the way, good morning."

"The same to you. I'll make some coffee, heat up the rolls, and bring them down."

The sheriff was waiting for Chase when he walked down to join him. "I'm sorry to wake you up so early, but we have a trip to take to the state penitentiary in Deer Lake. One of Gartner's men is willing to talk to us about what's happening up here. Or I should say, he wants to talk specifically to you."

"What are you talking about?"

They both turned when Allison came down with the coffee and rolls. "Have a seat, Sheriff?"

He grinned. "Is this a restaurant now?"

Allison smiled. "No, sir, it's just that I'll make sure you're taken care of properly."

The sheriff laughed. "I love this gal. Why haven't you married her?"

Allison smiled. "We're just business partners who are roommates temporarily."

"Yeah, right."

She smiled once more. "Enjoy a roll and have a cup of coffee." She took a seat at the table.

"Yes, ma'am," he grinned. The sheriff continued with what he was talking about. "Landon Rollins has been in the state pen for the past five years, and he said he knows you very well."

Chase nodded as he chewed his roll. "I represented him twice, and both times I got him off on a technicality. His luck must have run out."

"It sure did because he's spending twenty-five years in the pen for distributing and selling drugs in Montana. The drugs came from California, and Gartner was the man supplying them."

"What does it have to do with our Bigfoot?"

"We'll find out." The sheriff finished his roll. "Let's get going. It's a two-and-a-half-hour drive, and a snowstorm could be hitting us later today. I want to be back before it gets too bad."

"Ugh, I hate blizzards."

~

Later that morning, Allison's cell phone went off. It was her father. "Dad?"

"It is. I understand you're in Mountain Ridge, Montana."

"Yes, I am. How did you find that out?"

"A man named Nathan Shepherd called me and told me you needed me, so I came down as soon as I could. What's going on?"

Her face scrunched into a scowl. "I'm confused. Never mind, where are you? I'd love to see you."

"I'm probably twenty minutes from Mountain Ridge. I'm with a guy named Peter Drake."

"There's a bar and grill on Main Street which has wonderful food. We can meet there."

"That would be wonderful. It's been so long, sweetie."

Allison closed her cell phone. This made no sense at all, but she did miss her dad despite all that had happened in her life. It had been more than ten years since she'd last seen him. Based on his voice, perhaps he'd finally gotten his life together. She hoped so.

She walked over to tell Milo she was going to take a long lunch.

"I'll handle both sides until Xavier shows up."

"Thanks." She walked two blocks down to the bar and grill. The snow had started to fall lightly. She walked into the establishment and found a table where they could sit when her father arrived. Ten minutes later, Allison's father walked through the door with a tall man with dark hair and glasses.

She noticed right away that things had changed with her

father. He was clean shaven and wore a nice shirt and suit coat. Why was he here? She raised her hand when her father looked her way. He saw her, and the two hurried over to them.

Her father smiled. "Let me look at you, sweetie. You are gorgeous, your face is radiant, and you just seem so happy."

She hugged her father and nodded to the man with him. "I am, Dad. You look so much better yourself. Have a seat, and Jake will be over in a minute to take our orders."

They sat down. "This is Peter Drake. We're working on a project together that could benefit this area."

"The resort?"

Peter's eyes lifted. "You've heard about it? Of course, you would, if you're dating Willis Shepherd."

Allison sipped on her water. "We're not together anymore."

"I'm sorry," Peter said.

"I'm not."

They turned when Jake joined them. "Where's Chase today?"

"He's on his way to Deer Lake. What's the special today?"

"Grilled cheese and tomato soup. I'll grab some menus."

Once Jake left, Peter continued the conversation. "Are you talking about Chase Connor?"

"I am. Do you know him?"

"I do. It's a long story that I won't bore you with right now, but do you know when he'll be back?"

"He'll be back later. He's on his way to the state penitentiary with the sheriff to talk to some guy about our Bigfoot."

Drake lifted his eyes. "I have heard legends about Bigfoot in Montana. So there actually is one?"

Allison shrugged. "They caught a large guy over seven-foot who tried to drug Chase, so they believe he's the Bigfoot they've been looking for." She changed the subject. "Dad, why are you here?"

He sighed. "Peter can probably explain it better."

Allison eyed Peter Drake. "First of all, explain to me how you know Chase."

Peter smiled. "Good for you—you're very protective of the guy. Chase and I have known each other for several years. I know each of his family members, and he's the only one I would ever trust for any project."

Allison's eyebrows furrowed. "His parents are already involved, so what's the deal?"

"No, they're not involved with it. Nathan Shepherd believes they are involved with it, and that's where the problem comes in. The investors wanting this resort want nothing to do with the Connors, the Shepherds, or the Boyds, but they don't have the money to make it a go."

He stopped talking when Jake returned with the menus. They looked over the menus and ordered their meals. Allison stuck with the special and lemonade. The others ordered different meals with drinks. Once he left, Peter continued.

"Recently there was a meeting discussing the project, but nothing came out of it because Shepherd couldn't get the support he needed."

Allison took a deep breath. "I could say I'm sorry to hear that, but I'm not. It's about time Nathan gets what he deserves."

A small smile lit up Peter's face.

She turned to her father. "What are you doing now?"

He took a deep breath. "I work with Mr. Drake's company. We look for land and funding to build projects like this resort. I've been clean for three years now, and I'm slowly getting my life back together."

"I'm glad, Dad, but I don't know what I can do to help you in this situation." She stopped. "Unless you were thinking I could talk Chase into working with this group?"

Her father shook his head. "I didn't know anything about Chase Connor until you mentioned his name today. The only reason I came was because Nathan Shepherd said you needed me."

"How would you know him? Do you run in the same circles he does?"

"Correct."

They stopped as the food showed up. "This is quite a nice place," Peter said. "And if the food matches the prices, this is a Montana gem."

Chapter 26

Sheriff Portal and Chase stood at the entrance of the state penitentiary waiting for the bars to open so they could walk through. Once they opened, they walked into a room. There sitting at a table was a small man with long, greasy hair, bent wire-rimmed glasses, and tattoos over most of his exposed body.

"Chase Connor, it's so good to see you again. If I would have had you as an attorney, I wouldn't be here for the next twenty-five years."

Chase shrugged. "It was only a matter of time before you were behind bars."

He nodded. "You're right. My own stupid fault, but my goal while in here is to make amends—"

Sheriff Portal interrupted. "That's what all criminals say."

Landon eyed the sheriff. "From what I read, you've been able to solve some crimes that have infested your county for several years because of Chase and his books."

The sheriff glared at Landon. "Drop the BS and tell me why we're here."

Landon met his glare. "I told them I wouldn't talk to anyone but Chase. You can leave anytime."

The sheriff stood up. "This is a waste of time."

Once the sheriff left, Landon turned to Chase. "Is he always that wired?"

Chase grinned. "He's a good man, but he's tired of all the BS that criminals lay on him. Why am I here? You know I can't do anything to reduce your sentence."

He sipped on his cup of coffee that had been placed in front of him. "I know I'll die here, but hopefully not before I make a few things right. One of them is making sure Jonathan Gartner gets what he deserves. If he's stuck in this place with me, I can make sure he doesn't do anything to humans again."

Chase took a deep breath. "Say what you have to say."

"You're not going to believe me, but here it is. Ten years ago, there were three boys — all who have grown to more than seven feet tall. The Bernards, their parents, did nothing to help them, so Jonathan Gartner and another man, Zachary Bowdle, took them under their wings, taught them how to survive, how to kill, you name it. One of the boys broke into the Bernard house to search for a few million dollars in gold, which you found. Now the gold is on its way to Gartner's hands as we speak."

"How's that possible?"

Landon wheezed a bit. "The gold is being shipped from Kalispell to Helena tomorrow. Gartner knows the exact route, and there are a couple of spots that will cause problems for the truck, from which he plans on grabbing the gold. No one will live. That will include your sheriff friend or anyone who is with them. Then it's just a few miles to the Canadian border where he can cross over. He has dual citizenship, but more importantly, he knows all the hidden paths crossing into Canada."

Chase took a deep breath. "How does that fit into what's happening around Smith Lake?"

"You've caught one of the two men who have been handling the boys for Gartner. There is a second man and a third boy that hide out in the mountains. No one knows who the second man is until now. There is a man whose brother is an attorney in Mountain Ridge."

"You mean Dr. Boyd is involved?"

"No, it's his younger brother. Your father got him off on a charge of kidnapping the Native American girls, which was a mistake because now Boyd's come back with a vengeance. Jeremiah is the most brutal of the three brothers. He doesn't hesitate to kill anyone in his way even without the help of Boyd's brother."

"Do you know where he's located?"

"That's the tough part. Jeremiah has never been seen before. It's always been Joshua, so everyone thinks it's just him and everything is settled. It's not." Landon wheezed once more. "All the bones you've found are of people who have been mules for Gartner."

"Wow, that's sick. Really sick."

"It's worked effectively so far because no one has been able to find the drugs since the mules aren't alive. Of course, when they transport the drugs from California, they have no idea what happens to them once they reach the other states."

"All the drugs come from California?"

"From Mexico then through California. Your family knows about it, as does Dr. Boyd, and many others. There is a shipment coming in two days to the Smith Lake area."

"What happens to the drugs once it reaches that area? And why that area?"

Landon wheezed a third time, blood issuing from his lips. He grabbed a napkin. "Buyers are waiting at the Mountain Ridge Bar & Grill."

Chase's eyes widened. "The owner knows about this?"

"He doesn't but there is another a guy who is a major drug distributor in the county but has never been caught because the drugs are in and out before anyone can find out, usually during their half-price alcohol nights. No one has a clue the bar's a front for distribution of drugs. How they're distributed I don't know. I don't know who the man is either."

"Why Smith Lake?"

"It's so close to the Canadian border, which is in the middle of nowhere, so they can slip easily over. There's also an open water passage during the winter under the lake that allows drug distributors to make it to other locations in the area. It's a multi-billion-dollar enterprise as you can imagine."

Chase shook his head. "You can't pin any of this on Gartner."

Landon lifted his hand. "Gartner is going to be in the area in the next day or two for a big meeting for this new resort they're planning. There's a cabin near Smith Lake where he stays."

"Do you know where?" Chase's eyes lit up.

"All I know is that it's along a tree line in the northeast part of the lake."

"There are several cabins in that area."

"True, but there's only one cabin with an old lady who loves to entertain men who come to the area. That's where it starts."

Chase rolled his eyes. "Are you saying this lady draws men to the cabin, sleeps with them, and then hooks them up with Gartner?"

"That's the extent of it. Not an elaborate scheme."

Chase leaned forward. "Where did you get all of this information?"

Landon wheezed again. "I was part of it all for many years in California until I got busted here in Montana meeting with this lady. I happened to leave her cabin, had a busted taillight, and was pulled over by a deputy. He was about ready to let me go when that idiot, Gideon, came after him."

"Why would he do that?"

"All three of those creatures are into games, and he thought it was a game. Gideon escaped, but I didn't, and here I sit. As for the rest of the story, you can find it in that book you're reading."

"How would you know about that book?"

Landon grinned. "We have several readers in the penitentiary, and they've talked about the interesting books you have in that bookstore."

"Did the former owner know anything about what was happening?"

"Mr. Boer? Yes, he could have. That is, if he's still alive. You could talk to him, but most likely Gartner took care of him."

Chase ran his fingers through his long hair. "Why are *you* still alive?"

"Am I? You've noticed I've wheezed four times and will be dead soon enough with my tumor."

"Have you had it checked out?"

He took a sip of his coffee. "The doctors have said there is nothing they can do about it, so this is my last chance to make things right before I go. I know you find this hard to believe, Chase, but you're a bright boy, and I know you can read between the lines. Everything is in two books, and you have both of them. One is the mystery book and the other is *The Drug Epidemic in Montana* or something like that." Landon wheezed once more, spewing out more blood.

Chase jumped up to get some help. The security rushed in as Landon's head fell down on the table. He checked his pulse and looked up at Chase.

"He's dead."

On the drive back to Mountain Ridge, Chase was quiet thinking about all he had heard. He turned to the sheriff's voice.

"Do you believe him?"

"That's the third time you've asked me that, and I'll tell you for the third time, as crazy as it is, I believe Landon. The guy was a big-time criminal, but he was on his deathbed, and he wanted to make sure that his story was told. It was his way to make things right, I guess."

Sheriff Portal turned north on the last leg to Mountain

Ridge.

Chase spoke once more. "I hate these resort meetings, but the best chance to catch Gartner is during one of them. Do you know when the next one is?"

"I don't know anything about a meeting other than the one that was held the other night."

"Could he have been there? Does anyone know what he looks like? Other than me."

The sheriff shook his head. "I'll call the county-commission chair to see if she knows what's happening." He connected with her right away. He hung up, then glanced at Chase. "Tonight, the meeting is being held at—"

"The Boyds?"

The sheriff looked at him. "You guessed it."

"I really hate these things."

The sheriff laughed. "You don't have to go."

"Does anyone in the county know what Gartner looks like?"

The sheriff sighed. "Even if we find him, I just can't arrest him."

Chase grinned. "Once he sees me, he'll hightail it out of there, and if it's my guess, he'll go into hiding where he feels safe."

"Smith Lake." They both said together.

Chase turned to a text message that came through. He read it.

The sheriff grinned. "Your lovely lady?"

"Yep, her father is in town and so is Peter Drake."

The sheriff shrugged.

Chase smiled. "Peter Drake also knows what Gartner looks like." Chase texted Allison back.

The sheriff asked, "What did you tell her?"

"Get your sexiest outfit on because we're going to the ball."

Sheriff Portal let out a breath. "So much for a lasting relationship." The sheriff dropped Chase off at the bookstore.

Chase walked up the stairs, opened the apartment door, and stopped. Two men sat on the couch. When he regained his breath, he said, "Peter Drake, it's great to see you."

The tall man stood, and the two hugged. "And you too. How do you like the bookstore-and- antique-store world?"

"I enjoy it, but I'm sure you're not here to purchase books or antiques."

"Nope, but I do want you to meet someone."

The older man stood up. "Chase Connor, it's nice to meet you. I'm Ethan Winters, Allison's dad, but I haven't been much of a father to Allison or her sister."

Chase offered his hand. "You're here now when she needs you."

Winters' eyes widened. "I didn't expect a comment like that. Thought you'd tell me to get lost after not being there for her over the last ten years."

Chase waved a dismissive hand. "I trust Allison. If she didn't want anything to do with you, she would have never brought you here." He turned back to Peter. "What brings you here?"

"Things have changed big time since you left. You may have heard I don't work for your father anymore, but I started my own land-and-property acquisition company."

"I didn't know that. Are you here working with Shepherd and my family with this resort?"

"Oh gosh no, after the fallout with your father, I won't have anything to do with the Connors. However, there is a group of investors who are interested in building a resort around here, but they need a little help."

"What kind of help?"

"Essentially, they need sound information. Everything that has come our way has been misinformation, and the investors are ready to drop out and go somewhere else. Do you believe this would be a good spot for a resort?"

"I can't say for sure, but it must be if my father is

thinking about it. Certainly the Shepherds have been pushing hard for it. Maybe you'll find out more tonight. Now, if you'll excuse me, I need to talk to Allison." Before he left, he turned back to Peter. "I have to talk to you alone before we go."

Peter nodded. Chase knocked on Allison's door.

"If that's you, Chase, come in." When she saw him in the mirror, she spun around, stood, and hugged him. "You made it back," she said, planting a kiss. She stepped back. "Is everything okay?"

"Yes, and no."

She took his hand, and the two sat down on her bed. He lowered his voice. "You look adorable. Believe me you do, but I need your help."

"Of course, I'll help you anyway I can."

Over the next few moments, Chase explained to Allison what was said at the prison, and as he talked, he could see the color drain from Allison's face. Once finished, she sighed. "You want me to snuggle up to a known drug dealer?"

He sighed. "That's about it. And don't say anything to anyone about it."

"I won't. Did you meet my father?"

"I did. He seems to be a nice guy."

She nodded. "He was until he got hooked on drugs. Do you think he's changed? I want to have a relationship with him, but I don't want to be disappointed once more."

He put his arm around her. "I realize the last few weeks have been tough for you, and I hope that your father is clean." He thought for a moment. "You know he may be on the level."

She lifted her head to peer into his eyes. "Why would you say that?"

"Because Peter Drake would never be involved with someone who's doing something illegal. That's why he doesn't work for my father anymore."

She put her arms around his neck. "I hope you're right. Once this is over, you and I need to have a pointed conversation about where we're going with each other."

"I agree. In the meantime, be very careful. Gartner is a killer and is very dangerous, but it's the only way we can get him."

She kissed him. "When are you going to stop playing the hero? You know what happened last time when you tried to do that."

"You'll have plenty of protection."

"I'm not worried about me; I'm worried about you." She stood up. "Let's do this, before I chicken out."

Chapter 27

Allison took a deep breath as she walked into the community center. She stopped, took off her coat, and handed it to the doorkeeper. All eyes gravitated toward her as she sashayed through the door of the conference room. She knew how she looked in her strapless, long blue dress that covered her platform heels. Chase said this Gartner creep loved tall women with cleavage. Not this girl—that would never happen with anyone other than Chase.

She nonchalantly grabbed a drink off the tray, took a sip of her glass of wine, and surveyed the surroundings. Peter Drake winked at her. Chase had said Peter would be there to watch over her instead of Chase. Once Gartner saw Chase, he'd find a way out in a flash.

At least three guys walked up to Allison with the usual pick-up lines. "I'm sorry but I'm here for a specific person, and I think I see him now." Allison strutted toward the man who fit the description Chase had given her. She stopped abruptly when Willis headed toward the same man. "Damn it, he was going to ruin everything," she said under her breath.

Peter Drake made a bead toward Willis and started up a conversation. *Thank you, Peter.* Allison hurried over to Gartner, who was talking to a couple of men.

Gartner stopped talking once he saw Allison, his eyes stripping her from head to toe. What a creep! "You're a beautiful, tall angel. Where did you come from?"

Allison pasted on a smile and noticed he kept his eyes on her chest. She adjusted her dress a bit so he would see just a little more cleavage. The thought of the guy undressing her made her nauseous. "I knew you must be a man of importance, so I made a beeline straight to you. My name is Allison, and you are?"

"Jonathan. Jonathan Gartner. Would you like to join me in the annex for a breath of fresh air?"

"I'd enjoy it. I just got here, but it may be much better in a quieter place."

She took his arm and the two walked out into a small annex away from the main convention rooms of the community center. They sat down on a bench. "Are you interested in this resort?" Allison asked.

"I sure am. You could say I'm the one who's putting the deal together. And you?"

"I'm not sure yet. My family has an investment interest in the project, but I'm not sure if the resort is the way to go."

His eyes rolled. "Why?"

"I'm not a fan of games of chance. I want a sure thing."

Her comment must have hit its mark because his eyes lit up. "Another good quality of yours, ma'am. You see I don't get involved with anything by chance; the things I'm involved with are sure things. For instance, I'm sure you and I will walk out of this building tonight directly to my cabin where you'll be romanced beyond expectations."

"You have a cabin?"

"Yes, near Smith Lake. I'll take you there in the next hour after I complete some business here."

"I look forward to it," Allison said, trying to keep her composure since acid burbled up from her stomach. Why did she agree to do this for Chase? She was going to kill him when this was over.

"There's one of the guys I need to talk to right there. Excuse me." Gartner hurried over to the man.

Allison pulled from her bra the small camera that Peter Drake had given her and secretly snapped a couple of photos. She hadn't had time to focus the shots. Hopefully she'd managed to get a few good ones of Dr. Boyd's brother.

Gartner and the man he was talking to joined her. "Allison, this is Louis Boyd, one of my partners in the resort project."

Boyd grinned. "Allison Winters, what are you doing here? I had heard you had broken it off with Willis, but you probably got the better end of the deal if you're thinking of hooking up with Gartner."

Allison smiled. "I always go for the big shots. Willis was just wasting my space."

They all laughed. Gartner broke in. "You know this gal?"

"I do," Boyd said. "She's been dating Willis for the past two years, but something happened, and they broke it off."

"What was that, dear?"

Allison sipped her wine. "He beat me one too many times."

Anger darkened the man's eyes. He may be a drug dealer, but she could tell he didn't go for women being beaten. The worst thing was about to happen. Willis Shepherd was heading their way. *Where are you, Chase? Please get here quickly.*

"Oh, another one of my partners," Gartner said. His eyes froze. Allison turned her head to what he was looking at. Thank God, it was Chase. Gartner turned back to Allison. "I'm sorry I have to leave now. Something came up."

Boyd hurried out the door after him. Willis joined her. "What are you doing here, Allison? And with Jonathan?"

She didn't respond; she just kept her eyes on what was happening.

Willis shook his head. "Here I thought you were screwing Chase, but you're in bed with Jonathan Gartner. What a slut!"

Allison slapped him as hard as she could. "Go to hell." She fled to the nearest door and ran into Peter Drake, who pulled her out of the way. "Are you okay?"

"Just a bit scared. I just hope they catch him."

"Chase will."

"How do you know Chase?"

Peter took a deep breath. "I used to work for his father, but something went wrong, and he fired me. Chase saved my life."

"How did he do that?"

Peter's eyes searched the area. "Chase and Samantha are the best of a bad lot. If you ever see Micah and a man named Hampton together, it means someone is going to die. That's what almost happened to me, but Chase stepped in, and they backed down."

Her eyebrows furrowed. "Why would they back down to Chase?"

"Ma'am, the Connors are worth more than fifty-billion dollars. Chase inherited almost thirty-five billion of it from his grandfather's will after he passed away."

Allison sighed. "Chase wants nothing to do with that money."

Peter sipped his drink. "He doesn't, and you're the first person who's ever figured that out." He smiled. "That was a helluva slap."

~

Chase jumped into his Jeep and followed Gartner who had climbed into a car with Boyd. The sheriff's department was ready for whatever was about to happen. As Chase expected, the car drove toward Smith Lake.

Gartner had to realize Chase was behind him. What was his game?

As Chase drove close to the cabin, blue lights shone behind him. Why was the sheriff pulling him over? He complied, noting in his rear-view mirror the deputy rather than the sheriff walking toward him

Right in front of him, Gartner's vehicle had stopped, and the two in the car walked back toward Chase. Deputy Samuels pointed a gun at Chase. "You might as well get out because this is the end of the road for you."

Chase slid out of the car and laughed. "I should have known Gartner had someone inside law enforcement here in the county. Is Glen Allan also on your payroll?"

Gartner smirked. "Now, Chase, you know I don't divulge that type of information. I do want to know how you figured this all out. No matter, because I'll finally be rid of the one person who will blow the whole operation. Climb in the car in front, and let's go for a ride. I have a couple of people who would love to meet you."

Chase had no choice but to do what he asked. Once in the car, they drove toward the cabin, but instead of stopping at it, they drove past and stopped at an entrance to the lake a mile or so away.

Gartner took a deep breath. "I might as well tell you everything since this will be the end for you. Everyone will realize you died trying to solve a crime you had no business being involved with. How many times were you told to let law enforcement take care of it?"

"Not enough, it seems."

The deputy pushed him forward toward the northeast portion of the lake. Chase knew they were heading to the opening under the water. He'd get an in-person view of how and where they were distributing the drugs around the area.

"I knew that the opening was a connection somehow, but I wasn't sure."

"Simple," Gartner said. "There are tunnels underneath, as you can imagine, through which we're able to move to other locations without being seen. We had plenty of protection with the Bernard boys, although you knocked Joshua out of commission. Jeremiah is still around, and you should know he's pretty upset about the whole situation."

Chase didn't respond. He was too busy thinking of a

plan to get out of all of this. His only hope was the sheriff was around somewhere and wasn't part of the conspiracy. They walked to another cabin that was hidden well behind a group of rocks.

Waiting for them was Nathan Shepherd.

"Why doesn't it surprise me that you're involved, Shepherd? What is this all about?"

Gartner took a deep breath. "Simple, it's about $30 billion, the money you inherited from your grandfather. It has nothing to do with drugs or kidnappings; it's just money, as you well know."

"If I'm dead the money reverts back to my family."

There was laughter around him. Gartner sighed. "No, my dear friend, your grandfather said that if you should die the money goes to certain nonprofits—specifically, all the ones Nathan Shepherd has started. Over the last couple of years, I've been starting nonprofits for this purpose. Do you remember the words *Anders Nonprofit Organization*?"

"Yes, that's the name of the group my grandfather was associated with."

"Well as of a year ago, Nathan and Willis Shepherd became Anders Nonprofit Organization, so all the money drops into that bucket which will then become ours."

Chase sat down on a rock. "I have a few questions for you. Is the sheriff's department involved also?"

The deputy laughed. "Of course. All except that bumbling Sheriff Portal, who was only able to solve cases after you started reading the damn books. I've never seen such an inept law enforcement official as Portal."

This time Chase laughed. "Well, don't be surprised if that inept sheriff walks right over here and arrests all of you. But, Gartner, you're telling me that you're not involved with any drug sales in the county?"

"Oh hell, yes, I need some petty cash until the big mother lode comes along."

"What about the million dollars?"

Gartner growled. "It seems someone tipped law enforcement off that we were going after it. Needless to say, that didn't work out. No matter, we have you."

Chase grinned. "If you would have read a book, you would have been able to find a million dollars in gold in the Bernard house. I'm surprised that you wouldn't have known about it since you're supposed to be so close to the Bernard family."

A screech rattled the mountain.

Chapter 28

"Jeremiah is getting closer," Gartner said. "Your time is almost up."

Chase sighed. "Explain to me how this is all supposed to work. Jeremiah is going to kill me, you frame the giant for the murder, and get away scot-free?"

"That's the gist of it. I really don't know why you stopped being an attorney because you were very good."

They all turned when Willis Shepherd joined them. "Dad, I have no idea where Allison's father is."

Chase grinned at Willis. "Did Allison smack you like you did her the other night?"

"She'll pay for what she's done to me, but not until after I have the satisfaction of seeing Jeremiah tear you into pieces."

Gartner lit up a cigarette. "Any more questions?"

"Yeah, what does Allison's father have to do with all of this?"

He took a puff. "Now that's a good question. Initially, he worked for me as a drug dealer, but he got so messed up I had to let him go. However, since he did wonders for my bottom line, I refrained from putting him out of his misery. Then I found out he started working with Peter Drake and his new company, which provided me an 'in' to this resort." He blew out a ring of smoke. "The problem is Winters has a soft heart for his daughters and couldn't make good on his part of the deal. So we didn't get the names of Drake's investors in order to bring them into the fold. No matter, because you being that rich and dying soon would give us everything we need."

"Why this area?" Chase asked.

"It's a perfect area to conduct my business because it's only a few miles from the Canadian border."

Chase laughed. "It doesn't matter anyway, because once Jeremiah shows up, this will be all over one way or another. Who controls him?"

"Boyd, of course."

"And if something should happen to Boyd, what happens to Jeremiah?"

They all looked at each other. Gartner laughed. "We never thought about that. It will never happen."

Just like that, Chase dove toward Boyd, knocking his head into a large rock. Then he rolled and darted toward the mountains.

"Get the son of a bitch," Gartner yelled somewhere behind him.

Chase found a place to hide for a moment to catch his breath. He hoped hitting the rock knocked Boyd out or even killed him—long enough for Jeremiah to realize he was all alone once more.

The screech was much louder, meaning Jeremiah was close. A few moments later, Chase covered his ears at a screech that literally shook the earth. The minute Jeremiah found Boyd, all hell would break loose.

Over the next thirty minutes, he heard their voices but the darkness was Chase's only aide. He took a deep breath and made his way down another trail. He stopped when he heard the screech, this time followed by a scream. One gone. Without knowing it, Jeremiah was helping Chase.

Chase stopped when he heard footsteps. "I thought I saw him go up this way."

"Boss, why don't we just hightail it out of here?"

"Are you crazy? Willis, that guy has so much money and it's going to be ours."

"Not if that creature catches up to us."

"Jeremiah's down at the bottom of the mountain looking for us. We're okay up here."

They stopped at the sound of gunshots and voices down at the bottom of the mountain trail. "Damn it, the young Connor was right. The sheriff figured out something for the first time in his life. Let's find Connor and get the hell out of here."

Chase heard a familiar voice nearby. "Okay, Gartner, drop your weapon right now or I'll cut you down." Weapons thumped to the ground.

"Chase, you can come out now. The bad guys are all under control."

He stepped out from behind the rock. "Hamilton, Bro, it's great to see you. I'm sure Micah is here also." That brought a big laugh. "That's the Hamilton I remember." Chase turned toward Gartner. "You're the lucky one."

"Why?" Gartner asked.

"When my brother, Micah, and Hamilton are together, it means only one thing. Someone dies."

Approaching voices came from the mountain. The sheriff arrived with a couple of deputies. "Well, Chase, your plan worked. We have everything we need to convict these crazies. Take them away."

Hamilton and Chase were the only two left on the mountain. "What are you doing here?"

They turned to the loveliest vision Chase had seen in a while. Allison was trying to catch her breath.

"I'll let her explain. Glad you're alive." Hamilton gestured with a tilt of his head at the love of Chase's life.

She hurried over to him. "Oh my gosh, you're alive. I got here as soon as I could." Allison wrapped her arms around him and kissed him everywhere on the face.

"Slow down. What are you doing here?"

She stepped back. "Saving your life. What do you think I'm doing?"

"I don't understand."

Allison finally caught her breath. "When I was in California, I heard your father talking to Micah about this resort while they were having drinks. They mentioned the Shepherds and tonight's event. Your father asked me if I knew anything about it, and I told them everything I knew about the Shepherds."

"You were supposed to be resting in California, not spying."

She waved a dismissive hand. "Last night Samantha called me and told me that your brother and this Hamilton fellow were flying to Montana to help out. I didn't know what that meant, but she said to talk to Peter Drake, whom I didn't know until he showed up today with my father. He covered everything on this end until they got here. He's down there also with the sheriff's department. Not all deputies are crooked."

"Is Boyd alive?"

She grinned. "He has a hellacious headache, but he'll be okay."

Chase sat down next to her and took her hands. "Where's your father?"

She sighed. "He turned himself in and explained the whole story to the sheriff. Why would he do this?"

Chase wrapped his arms around her. "Your father was into drugs, and he worked for Gartner. He had no choice because if he didn't do it, Gartner would have killed the ones he cared about the most. Your father did it out of love for his two daughters.

"Is there any way you can help him?"

"Right now, let's join the others and see what we can do."

They arrived down to a crowd of law enforcement, who were arresting those involved.

The sheriff joined them. "I didn't get to tell you before, but I'm glad you made it out okay, but then I had no doubt you'd find a way to do it."

"What took you so long to get up there?" Chase asked.

He grinned. "I was waiting for the right time."

"Was the right time when Micah and the others arrived?"

They all laughed. The sheriff hugged Chase. "I heard what the deputy said about me being an inept sheriff, and he's probably right. Thanks for helping me out when you could. I'm sorry I almost cost you your life."

"You've always been there when I needed you, and you were again tonight."

They turned when Micah joined him. Allison hurried over to him and hugged Chase's brother. "Thank you for getting here in time."

"No, thank you for making us aware. As much as he pisses us off, Chase is still our little brother. I need to talk to him alone."

The sheriff took Allison's hand and walked away. "Are you okay?" Micah asked.

"I'm okay. Thanks for coming to the rescue. Like I told Hamilton, usually you two are on the other end."

"Yeah, sometimes it sucks, but we finally nailed a guy who should have been put away a long time ago. Samantha asked me to talk to you. We need you to come back to California and take over the business. Things have changed at the law firm, and we need to take a different course of action. Not the way it's going now, getting rich people off, letting criminals walk like Gartner. If he would have been put away when he should have, maybe none of this would have happened."

"I can't, Micah. This is my home now, plus I have found plenty of excitement in my books."

Micah laughed. "I can imagine. If you won't join us back in California, don't let Allison Winters go. She called me several times on the flight here telling me to hurry. If she'd been on the jet, I would have thrown her out of the back of the damn plane."

This time Chase laughed. He looked toward Allison and the sheriff. "I've made so many mistakes in my life, but losing Allison would have been the most devastating."

"Believe me, little brother, she'd marry you right now standing on this mountain." He started to walk away. "By the way, you can tell your beauty that her father will be just fine. We explained to the sheriff that he worked undercover for us trying to nab Gartner."

"Thanks, Micah."

"Anything for my little brother."

Once he left, Chase walked over to the sheriff and Allison. She smiled at him and linked her arm to his.

"What is our next adventure?"

The Sheriff and Chase laughed. "Hopefully, it will be awhile before anything exciting happens again."

Allison grinned. "I've known Chase since October, but I can tell you—with him there will always be an adventure."

Chase spent the next couple of hours at the Flathead County Sheriff's Department providing a statement on what happened during the course of the evening. Once he was finished, he walked out to the lobby where many were still sitting waiting to be questioned.

He sat down next to Allison and her father. Chase took Allison's hand. "I'm sorry I got you into this."

"Don't be. That's what people do when they love each other."

He eyed her. "I've said it a couple of times before, and I meant it each and every time. One day I'll have everything together, and we'll be just fine."

Her father slapped him on the back. "Chase, I'll never be able to thank you enough for what your family did for me. I screwed up many years ago being involved with Gartner, but I thought I was finished with him."

"It's okay. Make amends with your daughter." Chase stood up and kissed Allison on the forehead. "Enjoy your time with our father. I'm going home to bed."

"Good night."

"Good night." She smiled. "Don't be surprised if you get a phone call at seven in the morning."

Chapter 29

The next morning Allison woke up a little later than normal. She stared at her cell phone and saw it was eight so she couldn't call Chase and talk to him like he had done to her many times when she was in California. It didn't matter anyway because he was already on his way to Whitefish to pick up an antique bed.

She climbed out of bed, stripped down, and climbed into the shower. As she felt the warm water run over her body, she thought about what had happened over the last few months. Willis Shepherd was out of her life, and hopefully he'd be spending several years in prison with his father—a place they both deserved.

Her father was back in her life, and they had talked about taking a trip to see her sister in California. If Allison had known that her sister lived there, she would have found a way to find her when she was with Chase's family. Her sister was happily married with two children.

Allison wiped a tear out of her eyes wondering if she could have children. She had waited long enough and wanted to try to make love with Chase. It was time to move past what had happened to her with Willis. Chase would never intentionally hurt her, and she had so badly wanted to sleep with him since she'd returned from California.

Allison was drying her hair when the apartment buzzer went off. Who could that be? She pressed the intercom button. "Can I help you?"

"Yeah, your California bed is waiting for you."

"Wow, I wasn't expecting it today, but it's perfect timing. Can you give me a few minutes?"

"I'll wait right out here in the snow."

Allison quickly put on her pants. "It's snowing again?"

"Yeah, it's been like that all the way from Salt Lake City."

She finished putting on her sweater and hurried downstairs to open the door. Two men stood there stomping their feet to get warm. "I'm so sorry."

"No worries," the one with a red beard said.

His partner, who wore a hockey jersey, pointed toward the door. "Where do you want it?"

She cringed. "It's up a set of stairs. There's a bed in the room you'll have to take out."

"No worries. We'll get started if you show us where everything needs to go."

"This way please."

Allison pointed at the stairs. "I'm making some coffee if you would like some?"

"That would be wonderful," the hockey fan said.

They had the original bed out of the room within thirty minutes and were working on putting the bed in when Allison came into the bedroom with two cups of coffee. "I also brought some coffee cake I made, if you're interested?"

"That would be wonderful," Red Beard said. They joined her at the kitchen table.

"This tastes wonderful," his partner said. "Does it always snow here?"

She laughed. "Yes, the first few months of the year are snowy. Where are you from?"

"We're from California and have traveled through the snow once we reached Utah. I'll be glad to be back in the sunshine."

After they finished their snack, the guys finished putting

the bed together. She paid for the delivery, setup, and removal of the other bed. "Good luck heading back to California."

Once they left, Allison hurried downstairs to open the bookstore. It was a busy morning with people browsing through both the antique store and bookstore. During her lunch break, Allison made the bed that she had put in Chase's room. She dropped on it once it was finished. It felt so good.

She jumped up when her cell phone went off. "Chase, are you okay?"

"Yeah, I am. I may be back later than I thought. The person who had the antique was on his way back from Columbia, ran into a little snow, and slid into the ditch. He's okay, but he won't be back until later today, so I won't be home until dinner."

"As long as you're okay."

~

Once off the phone, Chase walked downtown to grab a coffee. He walked into a bar and sat down on one of the stools.

"What will it be?" the lady behind the bar asked.

"Just a coffee."

She grinned. "You'd be the first to want just coffee during a blizzard."

"Are you kidding me? Another blizzard?"

"That's what they're saying. You don't like blizzards?"

Chase held his coffee in both hands. "I can't say as I do. It seems like I've been stuck in several of them since I've been in Montana."

"Where are you from?"

He finally took a sip. "I'm from California originally."

She laughed. "It sounds like you got a little sidetracked coming through Whitefish, Montana."

"Not really, I stopped here to pick up an antique bed."

She smiled. "Now that sounds tempting."

Chase almost spit out his coffee. "You wouldn't be able to sleep on it. It's an old bed that would fall down as soon as you touched it."

She finished wiping out a glass and putting it on the rack. "Are you a traveling antique dealer?"

Chase laughed. "No, I own a bookstore and antique store in Mountain Ridge."

Her eyes lit up. "Wow, Chase Connor. Everybody knows who you are. You're the guy who reads books and solves mysteries."

"I run a bookstore and antique store, that's it. And I help the sheriff when he needs it."

She leaned on the bar. "Have you thought about the mystery hunt?"

Before he answered, he asked her for a bag of chips. She handed him a bag. "What is the mystery hunt?"

"Each year…wait a minute, they're doing it two times this summer. Anyway, at the highest mountain range in the county, a group of people go to several cabins to search for some item. Nobody knows what item until the hunt starts. Anyway, no one has found the item they're looking for because either the people go missing or they run away scared."

He stared at her. Was she telling him the truth? It sure seemed like she was sincere. "I've never heard of such a thing."

"Many haven't because the sheriff's department doesn't want anyone to know about it. They say there's even a journal out there that someone put together that tells the story of what happened to the first group ten years ago."

"Interesting. Where did you hear about this?"

She sipped on a soda before she spoke. "I have a cousin who was asked to participate but decided against it, but he heard about it from the others who participated. I can give you his name if you wish?"

"Why not? It's something I can pass on to the sheriff."

"Here's his name. The sheriff and his deputies won't touch the area at all. In fact, no one goes up there anymore except those who participate in the mystery hunt. One is happening in June and then another in August."

Chase stuck the name and phone number into his pocket. He turned when an older man with bent glasses walked in.

"Are you Chase Connor?"

"I am."

"I'm sorry about everything, but I have the antique bed if you want to take it. You had better hurry because the blizzard is about ready to hit."

Chase dropped a ten spot on the bar. "Thanks for the company," he said.

She smiled. "Anytime. And if you're back again, don't forget to stop by."

The two guys hurried out the door. Chase followed the man to his house. Twenty minutes later they had stowed the bed in the back of the Jeep. Before he left, Chase texted Allison that he was on his way.

Chapter 30

Allison helped Chase carry the antique bed into the showroom.

"We'll worry about it tomorrow," Chase said. "I hate blizzards."

She took his hand. "I have something special for you tonight."

He eyed her. "What could that be?"

She smiled. "You'll find out."

He started to take off his coat.

"No need to." She took his hand, and the two hurried out to the Jeep.

He frowned. "You're acting weird."

She laughed. "Probably, but this is important to me."

The two drove toward Smith Lake. She was holding his hand, then told him to stop, and pull over. He rolled his eyes. She took a deep breath, and took off her coat, then she slipped off her sweater, and then unsnapped her bra. "A few months ago, we were in this exact same place. You told me no, and I've been saying the same thing to you because of what happened between me and Willis. I'm not afraid anymore, and I want to start from scratch." She leaned over and kissed him. "I've wanted to do this for several months and now I'm ready. Let's revisit the back of your Jeep."

The two climbed in the back, and although the wind blew outside the Jeep, the inside was warm and cozy. He gazed at her. "Are you sure you're okay?"

"Remember, this is my idea." She rolled on top of him once more, and the two made love for another hour. She sighed, melted in his arms, and lifted her eyes to him. "From the first time I saw you in October, I started to fall in love with you, but there was Willis and your girlfriends. I didn't want to ever be that girl who stole another man from someone."

A few moments later, Chase laughed when she was snoring lightly. He pulled the blanket over her and the two spent the night in the Jeep. Early the next morning Chase opened his eyes when the sun hit him. Allison was still sleeping.

He shook her gently, and her eyes popped open.

She yawned and stretched her arms. "I'll remember last night for the rest of my life."

The two got dressed and drove toward the bookstore in a foot of snow.

"Wow, I didn't know it snowed that much," Chase said.

"No worries. We don't have anything to do today since the stores are closed. Besides, I have a surprise for you."

"Another surprise?"

She giggled. "I hope you like it."

It was after seven when they arrived back at the bookstore. They climbed up the stairs. "I'll make us some blueberry pancakes, which are your favorite, but you have to help me."

"Okay," he said.

Chase stirred the batter while Allison grabbed the blueberries to mix in it. She came over and dumped them in, while Chase continued beating the pancakes. When she turned toward him, Chase smeared some batter on her face. She laughed and did the same thing to him. Minutes later, the room was a mess, their hair was mottled with batter, and their clothes needed a wash. Chase looked at her. "We don't have much left for pancakes."

They cooked what was left and sat down to eat.

Chase gazed at her. "The pancakes were wonderful. Where did you learn how to cook?"

She fluffed her hair. "I'm not just a beauty, I do have other qualities."

"Like what?"

"Well, as you've seen, I'm pretty good in the water and on the volleyball court, and I'm a good card player."

"Okay, I'll give you all of those."

She set the plate back down on the table, then climbed onto his lap, and kissed him. "And as you also know," she said, batting her eyes, "I can also handle myself in a Jeep."

He grabbed her hand. "What's really going on?" Chase asked.

She took a deep breath. "I've been thinking about everything that has happened the past few months, and especially the past couple of weeks. I'd be a total mess if you weren't in my life."

She climbed off his lap. "I have one more surprise for you. Please give me a few minutes and then come into the bedroom you sleep in."

Five minutes later, Allison opened the bedroom door, sticking her head through it. "I'm ready."

He opened the door and looked inside.

"Ta-da," she said.

His eyes opened wide. "What did you do?"

She grinned. "This is the bed I love sleeping in, and I've wanted to sleep with you, so figured since we were going to start a life together, we should do it in style." Allison wrapped her arms around him and kissed him. "What do you think?"

"I think this is cool."

She smiled. "I did my job. Now for the finale, this is something I bought when I was in California—specifically for the first time in this bed. She took off her robe, revealing her negligee.

His eyes widened even more than before. "I can see everything."

She giggled. "Correct, from this moment forward, everything you see right now will be yours." She took his hand, pulled down the sheets, and undressed him. She slipped off her negligee and climbed into bed with him. "I've wanted to spend a day with you like this, and it is going to happen today." She giggled. "But first, I really have to go."

She jumped off the bed, raced into the bathroom, and came out a few moments later. "Now where were we?"

Several hours later, Allison rolled away from Chase. She grabbed her cell phone, noticing it was close to noon. "I'm hungry. I'll make us something." She grinned. "Oh wait, I've already taken care of that." Allison grabbed a plate of grapes, strawberries, and cantaloupe.

He smiled. "You think of everything." He popped a grape in his mouth. Chase grinned and rolled over to her.

It was dark outside, and they still held each other in bed. "This was a wonderful idea spending the day in bed while there's a blizzard outside," Chase said.

She rolled into his arms. "Would you be disappointed if we never could have children?"

He shook his head. "I wouldn't be because I have you, but I won't give up hope, and neither should you."

She laid her head on her arm. "I remember many times when it would be snowing, and my sister and I would play in the snow—make a snowman and throw snowballs at my parents while my mom was still alive. It's one of the few memories I have of my family. When my mother died, it seemed all that fun disappeared. What kind of memories do you have?"

Chase thought about it. "Micah, Samantha, and I would run along the beach in front of our home in San Diego. A lot of times there were races, but even being the youngest, they let me hang with them."

"That sounds like so much fun. Did you know that

Olivia is still in love with you?"

"Yeah, I know she is, but I don't feel the same way about her. She is a doll, and I don't know how she puts up with Micah, unless she doesn't know what he does."

She eyed him. "And what exactly does he do?"

He gently stroked her hair. "Micah's main job in the Connor family is to find business clients for Dad and the board. At times he can get mean, especially when Hamilton is with him. Everyone involved with the most recent scheme was fortunate."

Allison sighed. "I believe in true love, and I have a feeling that's what we have. Nothing ever breaks true love apart."

"Maybe so." He took a breath. "Samantha is married and has two children. They lived together for several years before they finally got married."

"It sounds like that's what you want to do, live together."

He climbed out of bed.

"Where are you going?"

He opened the top drawer and grabbed something. After crawling back under the covers, he opened the box in front of her eyes and slid a blue-stoned ring surrounded by diamonds onto her left hand. "This, my dear, is a Montana sapphire ring."

Her eyes went wide. "What does this mean?"

"It means I would rather marry you than live with you."

~

It was past ten that evening, and Allison couldn't sleep—probably because they'd been in bed all day. She came out onto the couch and pulled a blanket over her. There she sat staring at the ring. Chase hadn't asked her to marry him but had hinted about it. Allison turned when she heard the bedroom door open.

Chase slid down beside her. "I couldn't sleep either."

She nodded. "I was sitting out here thinking about this

ring and what you said. I mean, you said that you would rather marry me than live with me, but you didn't actually ask me. You just put this beautiful Montana sapphire ring on my finger. Am I right in assuming it's not an engagement ring? What does this mean exactly?"

He kissed her hand. "If you want an engagement ring, I'll purchase you one, but the whole idea behind this ring was to give it to the woman I'm in love with. I know it's you I'm in love with."

"I needed to hear those words," she said, pulling him down onto the couch with her. In order to fit, she had to lie on her side with her leg and arms around him. She kissed Chase. "I'm in love with you also. Today was such a lovely day, and I want to sleep all night in your arms."

The next morning Allison jumped at Chase's cell phone.

"Hello." Chase listened to what was said and then closed it.

Allison peered up at him. "Who was that?"

Chase took a deep breath. "Gartner."

"What did he want?"

Chase was quiet before he spoke, his lips in a single line. "He said, 'the games are just beginning.'"

THE END

Other books by this author
Hidden in the Book, Map of the Lost, Book 1
Bouncing Back
The Battle Off the Court
Freedom Flight
Fight for Survival
Road to Hell
A New Life Begins
Relentless
Missing
Targeted

Author Bio: My wife, Susan and I have two sons, Justin (Kayla) and Jeremy and a grandson, Aiden. Born and raised in South Dakota. I enjoy spending time with family, traveling and putt-putt. I recently retired as managing editor of a small town Iowa newspaper. I am a former Marine Corps veteran, getting my start in the publishing business in 1981 working for several years on base newspapers. I spent time running my own freelance business. I love writing. I enjoy reading anything and everything. I also love the history of our country and enjoy reading western books, mysteries, and adventure novels, and watching mystery, adventure, and western movies.